Forbidden Fruit

A Novel

Sandy Shavers

This book is a work of fiction. Any references or similarities to actual events, people (living or dead), or locales are intended to give he novel a sense of reality. Any similarity to other names, characters, places, and incidents is entirely coincidental. All poems are the original work of the author.

ISBN: 0615515916
ISBN 13: 9780615515915
Library of Congress Control Number: 2013916427
CreateSpace Independent Publishing Platform
North Charleston, South Carolina

for Shay

1

Tonya sat looking out the window of her newly decorated recreational room in her four-year-old home. She had encouraged her husband Keith put in a skylight and a bay window to bring more light into the room. She sat admiring the fresh paint job she had done on her own; His since she couldn't get Keith to complete the much-needed project, she was up for the challenge. To give the illusion of a larger space, Tonya chose a light color for her ceiling and walls, without contrast. She had debated between argent or eggshell but decided on alabaster, which contained a hint of blue. She enjoyed spending quiet moments in her new sanctuary, which she used as her safe haven to escape the pressures of life. The light from the window brought tranquility to the room. Given the amount of time she spent here, this was by far her favorite room in the house.

Tonya spotted her neighbor, Larry Tyler in his front yard, tediously pulling at the weeds that grew under his feet. *Today is as good as ever,* she thought, as she looked toward the sky and saw the feathery clouds as they lightly bounced along. She reminisced about how she'd wished she could touch the clouds when she was a little girl. She had imagined the feeling of soft, fluffy cotton sifting through her tiny fingers, as she pulled them to her mouth and how they tasted like cotton candy. She remembered the urge of wanting to run and jump from cloud to cloud as she delicately touched each one. She'd effortlessly soar above her house, looking down and having no fear of falling back to earth, because the clouds could sustain her weight. Today's weather made her want to run outside and enjoy the welcoming warmth of the sunrays on her skin. It apparently made Mr. Tyler tend to his lawn.

Tonya felt like a nosy neighbor as she sat watching her neighbors go about their daily tasks. The unsuspecting man hadn't the slightest clue that he had a spectator. Tonya always referred to Larry Tyler simply and respectfully as "Mr. Tyler," despite his persistent requests to be addressed by his first name. Mr. Tyler, a recent widower, was watering his lawn, which appeared to be already well hydrated. For a man who was more than seventy years old, he looked to be in pretty good shape. Tonya didn't have a physical attraction toward Mr. Tyler but the manner in which he carried himself did grab her attention. She noticed how the elderly man's pants were always pressed, with a thin, crisp crease down the middle; his shirts were starched to perfection; and his face was always clean-shaven. It was if his wife had never left.

Mr. Tyler had lost his wife of thirty-two years, Carol, two years ago to a massive heart attack. Carol had never been sick or complained of chest pain, so the death had taken the entire family by surprise. She was a retired schoolteacher who had spent most of her days caring for her two rambunctious grandchildren. The children often ran and played in the yard with such exuberance, that after an hour one would think they'd be tired out. Tonya wished for just a ray of the energy they'd possessed. If she could bottle up the energy from those young tots, she'd be relentless. Carol Tyler was the first neighbor Tonya had the opportunity to meet when she and Keith had moved into their new home. She was so friendly and thoughtful, bringing lunch when she came over to the house to introduce herself to the young couple. The Tyler's had only one child, Janine worked as a physical therapist and recently had gotten a job at a local hospital to be closer to her parents. Tonya remembered Janine coming over on the weekends to visit her parents, but she never gave more than a half smile, a quick wave of her hand, and a simple "Hello" to Tonya from across the street.

After Carol's death, Mr. Tyler elected to remain in the family home, despite his daughter's insistence that he move in with her and her family. He felt it was imperative that he remain in the home, as it was closer to where his beloved wife was buried. The couple was young when they had decided to move into their home and start a family. Carol had just graduated from the University of Alabama with a degree in childhood education, and he had been on the police force for five years when they had found what they referred to as their "love nest." The following year, Carol gave birth to their only child.

Being a retired police officer, Mr. Tyler was much too proud to be taken care of by someone else. Why should he burden his daughter when he could care for himself? He was quite independent, even caring for Carol five years earlier when she had fallen and fractured her hip. From where Tonya sat, he looked to be doing a pretty good job. Janine was faithful in checking on her father, helping him with his household chores, and making sure he kept his doctor's appointments. After he had proven to her that he could manage without her constant assistance, Janine stopped pestering her father about moving in with her and her family; besides, he was adamant about staying in his home.

2

Tonya Lacey Paris thought about the love of her life, Keith Paris Jr., affectionately known as "K.J." A hint of a smile creased the corner of her mouth, as she reminisced about the day she'd met the overly confident young man she had loved to hate until he'd found her heart. Tonya had met Keith in her junior year of high school. He was tall, dark, handsome, and very athletic, making him easy on the eyes. He also was well known at school, mainly because he was on the basketball team, a point guard whose number was thirty-three. Tonya's first impression of Keith was that he was a pretty boy who liked to showboat on the court. He had all the girls' attention, and not once did he look Tonya's way. Why should he? He was the center of attention. Standing six foot four, towering at least six inches over most of the boys in his class, and with pronounced muscles in his thin arms and legs, he looked every bit the part of a basketball player. His good looks and charisma, which made him all the more appealing, made it was clear to anyone who met him that he was a superstar in the making—perhaps the next Kareem Abdul-Jabbar, the Lakers' center who also had worn number thirty-three on his jersey. Tonya wasn't blind to the fact that Keith was eye candy. She saw why the girls were going crazy over him.

One girl in particular Tonya saw Keith with on a daily basis was a pretty petite cheerleader named Rain who believed the universe evolved around her Tonya thought it didn't help when others treated her like a celebrity. Rain's dad was some air- force big shot, and her mom was a music teacher who often gave voice and piano lessons in her home. Rain was an only child who was beyond spoiled rotten. She prevented all the girls from even looking at Keith, because she had her name written all over him, but that never stopped Keith from looking at other girls. Rain had a jealous mean streak, which became quite evident when any girl attempted to show Keith attention. After a game, Rain once drenched a freshman with soda when she had walked up and congratulated Keith on his team having won the game.

One night, after another game, Keith approached Tonya as she was on her way to meet her friend Shelia, who was on the same cheerleading squad as Rain.

"Hey, how'd you like the game?" Keith blurted out, sticking out his chest to show his confidence, and smiling, which revealed those deep hollow pits in his cheeks.

Tonya looked at Keith askance before answering. *Well, isn't he full of himself!* she thought. She let out a deep sigh. "It was a good game."

"What did you think of the star player?" Keith asked with a smirk.

Tonya glared at him. Oh, how she'd love to slap that smirk right off his face.

"Oh, Steve was just great! Did you see that slam dunk he made?"

Instead of being upset about the insult, Keith laughed. "I guess I deserved that."

Tonya noticed the deep-brown color of his eyes, which sparkled when he smiled. It sent a chill down her spine which frightened her. How could she maintain her composure or senses if she ever fell deeply into those eyes? His eyes were so mesmerizing that she couldn't tell if they held truth or lies, because she couldn't see past the curtains that covered the windows to his soul.

Extending his hand to Tonya, Keith purred, "Hi, I'm Keith."

Tonya took his hand and shook it briskly. "I know who you are. I'm just not impressed with conceited guys." *The nerve of this guy acting like he just got a million-dollar NBA contract,* she thought, *when he's only playing high school basketball.*

"I'm not conceited. I just know who I am."

"And who might that be?" Tonya twisted her mouth into a contorted smirk of her own.

"Stick around, and you might find out!"

For the next three weeks, Tonya avoided Keith; she didn't like the way he looked at her. He made her feel as if she were a piece of prime steak. Tonya had been brought up in a Christian household and knew what the devil looked like when she saw him, and Keith Paris had "Satan" written all over him.

Her mother always told her about wolves in sheep's clothing and how the devil walks the earth seeking out those he can corrupt and devour.

Tonya's father was a minister who preached the word of God and expected his children to be living examples of the word he preached. Tonya and her sister Carmen had grown up without their mother, who had died at age thirty-three from ovarian cancer. Tonya was ten years old, and Carmen was seven when they lost their mother and had to be raised by their father and members of the church. The overzealous women of the church whom the girls mostly encountered wanted nothing more than to get closer to Elder Lacey, only accepting his two young daughters as part of the package deal. One of those women was the unforgettable Sister Linda Barrett.

Tonya remembered Sister Barrett coming over to bring hot meals for her family shortly after her mother had passed away. Sister Barrett was a young, slim, very attractive single woman with a knock-out body and a beautiful smile. She was nice to both girls—that is, until Elder Lacey told her to stop coming over. Tonya vividly remembered the day her dad had sent Sister Barrett on her way when she once again had showed up at the house wearing provocative clothes in an attempt to entice him. Some church woman she turned out to be—more like a lioness awaiting her prey.

Tonya reflected on the evening Sister Barrett had showed up wearing a way-too-short black miniskirt and a low-cut blouse. The woman repeatedly had leaned over when she talked, which revealed her ample bosom, and the small butterfly tattoo on her left breast. She always cunningly dropped her pen, notepad, or napkin, trying anything to give Tonya's father a private show of her thighs and round buttocks under whatever short skirt she'd chosen to wear. Elder Lacey would all but cry out to God openly. That night, after Sister Barrett had given Elder Lacey her routine show of revealing some part of her anatomy, he began to pray for God's unchanging hand. Sister Barrett interpreted this as Elder Lacey's way of being spiritual, and jumped up and down like she had caught the Holy Ghost. Elder Lacey uttered thanks for the Lord's staying power, then politely escorted Sister Barrett to the door and whispered to her to never cross its threshold again.

After that night Tonya and Carmen never saw Sister Barrett at their home again or at church for that matter. The girls were glad for that, because although she was beautiful, she couldn't cook to save her life. Everything she cooked tasted like soap or a dog's dry chew toy. Tonya recalled the casserole Sister Barrett had cooked for the church's anniversary dinner. Most people in the congregation knew she couldn't cook, so the dish was left untouched. When she walked past and saw it still sitting on the table, she asked why no one was trying.

"Maybe they're not ready to meet their maker!"

"I hope they got their insurance paid up!"

Overhearing the servers whisper to each other, Tonya and Carmen giggled like little girls. Tonya was sureSister Barrett had heard the comment, but she continued to leave her dish out without showing an inkling of having heard their jeers.

Sister Barrett grabbed a big spoonful of her casserole, placed it on a plate, and handed it to Deacon Foster. "Here, Deacon. Have some of my casserole," she said, smiling as she leaned in to give him a view of her bosom.

With a deep frown, Sister Foster pushed the plate away from her husband, not attempting to hide her displeasure. "No casserole for him. He's watching his diet."

"Well, I'd hate to see it go to waste," Sister Barrett said.

Sister Foster rolled her eyes. "Chile, why did you make that mess when you knew no one would eat it? Some people should just stay out of the kitchen. Know yo' calling, chile, and know yo' place."

Sister Barrett placed a hand on her hip, looked at Sister Foster with sheer indignation, and stormed off.

Tonya wondered whether Sister Barrett was one of those wolves in sheep's clothing her mother used to talk about in her Sunday-school lectures.

Her parents had married right after high school and had started a family immediately. Bethany Lacey was a beautiful, slender-built, fair complexioned woman who loved her husband and children but whose life was cut short in its prime. Bethany was active in the church, singing in the choir, teaching Sunday school, and working in the church's office. She always told her daughter that God came first then family. This had stuck with Tonya even in her own marriage.

After Bethany was diagnosed with cancer, she became incapacitated. Her illness left her unable to do any of the things she loved to do for her family. Spending most days lying in bed and not with her family left her depressed. Chemotherapy drained her of her strength and made her sick for days at a time. The radiation therapy burned her until she was three shades darker than her usual almond color. After months of chemotherapy and radiation, Bethany decided to discontinue all treatment and live the remainder of her life spending quality time with her family.

She tried to encourage her husband to consider finding a mate to help him raise their two girls, but Elder Lacey would never make that promise to her. He didn't think his wife could ever be replaced, because he truly believed Bethany was his soul mate. Elder Lacey always kept Bethany's pictures on the walls throughout the house, which sometimes made other women feel uncomfortable when they visited. They often said they felt as if Bethany was watching them while they visited Elder Lacey.

After the death of his wife, Elder Lacey refused to remarry. He never even dated, believing that dating would open a door that would be impossible to close. When deacons and other ministers pressured him to remarry, he'd tell them his wife was his first love and was irreplaceable, so no matter how hard Sister Barrett or the other women tried, they never could reach his heart. After ten years of trying, but only getting Not for Sale sign from Elder Lacey, many of the women gave up and either relocated to other churches or turned their attention to more available men.

3

Tonya attended New Covenant Full Gospel Church, often referred to simply as "New Covenant," which was under the leadership of Pastor Willie Mullin. New Covenant was the only church that Tonya knew, since this is where her parents had been married and had raised their girls. This is where Tonya worshiped proudly and where she sang in the choir. When the choir was invited to sing at Mt. Sinai Baptist Church, led by Pastor Steve Mitchell, sixteen year old Tonya was more than willing to go.

After the choir had sung and gone to its assigned seating area, the next choir got up to sing. That's when Tonya saw the nightmare of her life. In the tenor section of the choir was none other than Keith Paris. He was singing and flashing that million-watt smile at her as she sat staring at him with her mouth wide open.

Carmen, Tonya's younger sister, leaned over and whispered, "Tonya, close your mouth before you catch a fly."

"Huh?" Tonya mumbled.

"Girl, you act like you've seen a ghost."

Carmen had no idea—it was worse than a ghost; it was that proverbial wolf, and he had traded his sheepskin for a choir robe.

That was eight years ago. After much thought, reconsideration, and overcoming Rain's rage, threatening phone calls, and stalking, Keith and Tonya began to date and eventually married. Tonya recalled their first date in the summer of 1994, when Keith had taken her to see the movie *The Lion King*. A lot had happened that year that made the year very significant in her memory. Earlier that year her father had urged the church to pray because a terrible tornado had hit a church in Alabama, killing twenty-two people. The church held shut-ins and around-the-clock prayer. It wasn't the only storm that year to devastate a large group of people. In November, Hurricane Gordon r r ipped through the Caribbean and the Southeast United States, killing more than 1,100 people. The church prayed even harder that the upcoming year wouldn't be as cruel.

Rain was no longer the pretty, prissy, and petite goddess she thought herself to be but had become the "Lady of Rage." Always her own biggest fan, she hated losing to anyone. She had started spreading lies about Tonya around school, but even that didn't deter Tonya and Keith from growing closer.

Rain drifted from one player on the basketball team to another. By the middle of the school year, she had found out she was pregnant and left school after the birth of her child. She never forgave Tonya for coming between her and Keith. From time to time, Tonya saw Rain around town, but each encounter was as cold as the last. Although Rain never spoke to Tonya, she did give her dirty "you stole my man" looks. Life hadn't been too cruel to Rain; she had maintained her figure and even wore her hair in a short cut that fit her face, but she was still bitter about her breakup with Keith and wanted Tonya to know that things hadn't changed between them. Tonya tried to take a peep at Rain's daughter, but when Rain caught her looking at her child, she quickly shielded her and whisked her away. Trying to avoid the sunlight, that glared down on her, Tonya was able to see the tiny face of the child Rain tightly held on to. The little girl looked just like Rain when she was younger, but there was something awfully familiar about the child's eyes.

Keith had been very romantic when he and Tonya were newlyweds. He'd surprise his young wife with candlelit dinners, welcoming bubble baths, and love letters and poems he often left on her pillow. He was a poet at heart and often shared his work with Tonya or dedicated a poem to her. The romance lasted for the first three years of their marriage. By the fourth year, however, Keith spent more time out with the boys, and Tonya spent more time at church. "God before family," her mother always had told her.

Tonya now reflected on her husband's affectionate gestures during the early years of their union. Keith had been very thoughtful and caring toward her. He'd kept her blushing like a teenage girl with his heartfelt tokens of love and admiration. He'd made her feel as if she were the only woman who mattered, and Tonya had been in heavenly bliss. She believed Keith would put the world on hold just for her. She remembered a poem titled, "Chestnut Brown" that he had written for her while they were dating. The poem was both touching and unforgettable.

Chestnut cool and cocoa breeze.
I dare to stare into your brown
eyes, so deep they are sure to please.
Eyes so surreal that they read my mind.
Eyes so hypnotic that they touch my soul.

I fidget and glare but dare not stare
into that welcoming place of serenity,
just to know what truth they hold,
just to know they touch my soul.
My mind, my heart, my inner me
are ready to slip, ready to fall into those
easy, breezy, beautiful eyes
to a place of peace and tranquility,
just to know you reached my soul
with your chestnut cool and cocoa breeze.

Tonya knew that one of the major problems in her marriage was the fact that her husband wanted children, and for the past eight years, she hadn't been able to become pregnant. She'd had several false alarms, thanks to modern-day pregnancy tests. Pink means positive? Two lines mean positive? One line means negative? It was all so confusing.

Keith eventually withdrew and stopped trying. Feeling helpless and hopeless, Tonya jumped full force into anything that would take her mind off the possibility of her womb being barren and left it all up to chance.

One day, while speaking to Sister Peggy about her problem, she was advised to "let go and let God," and that's exactly what she did. She prayed an earnest prayer that God would give her a child. *Lord, you worked miracles for women in the Bible like Hannah and Sarah. I need you to do the same for me. I'll dedicate my child back to you as Hannah did.* Tonya knew God heard her prayers; she just didn't want to be like Sarah, too old to enjoy her baby, even with modern medical advances. *I can't do what Sarah did!* she thought, as she ended her daily talk with the Lord. Elder Lacey had taught her to pray specifically for what she wanted. Tonya heeded her father's words and prayed for her heart's desire, as she knew God would keep his promises if she kept her mind on Him.

Sister Peggy Frazier was the pastor's secretary and had been a member of New Covenant for as long as Tonya could remember. She was always shouting crazy sayings that left the church roaring with laughter. One Easter Sunday morning, after the choir sang one of Sister Peggy's favorites, "Celebrate,"she jumped up and danced and shouted until her knee-high stockings became anklets. For a woman of 280 pounds, Sister Peggy had more moves than all the young people of New Covenant combined. One of her favorite sayings was "Drop-kick me, Jesus, through the goal poles of life!" which was usually followed by her falling face-first to the floor. It almost always took a few ushers and deacons to help Sister Peggy off the floor once she got in the spirit and felt the need to be "dropped-kicked" by Jesus.

Sister Peggy had three daughters who lived in different parts of the world. Her oldest daughter, Sharon, was married to a navy officer and traveled a lot, never living in one place for long. Her middle child, Lisa, had moved away after high school. She finished college and began her career as a social worker. Sister Peggy's youngest daughter, Felicia, was a high school senior who was still at home. Sister Peggy often referred to Felicia as "the last pea in the pod." Sister Peggy was forty-two when Felicia was born, and she thanked God for her miracle baby, because she'd thought her days of changing diapers were well over. Sister Peggy's husband, Deacon Ralph Frazier, was a retired fireman who was mild mannered but very dedicated to the church, much like his wife. Deacon Frazier didn't look like a typical fireman. He was a petite man, but his stoic manner made up for his size. It took a lot to ruffle Deacon Frazier's feathers, but one thing he couldn't stand was disrespectful and unruly children.

Tonya reflected on one of the few times Deacon Frazier had let loose in church. When she was around twelve years old, during a regular Sunday service, she happened to sit next to the wrong person and apparently on the wrong day. Tonya remembered attending church with the Lee family. George and Barbara Lee had a nine-year-old son, Stanley, who was known for his antics. Stanley was always talking and playing in church, which wasn't allowed. The ushers often stationed themselves next to his pew just to keep an eye on him. They always stood scowling and looking down on the children wagging a finger in their faces, as if it were their given task. The children were often told they should be seen and not heard, so Stanley knew a rebuke was soon coming. One of the elderly women, Mother Smith, frowned at him, pursed her lips, and let out a loud "Shhh!" Stanley immediately got angry at being reprimanded and promptly told Mother Smith to get her butt checked because she had sprung a leak. Mother Smith gasped loudly and clutched her chest, shocked at the young boy's response. The church became still, as the unsuspecting child had committed the ultimate sin of disrespecting his elder. Word of the offense quickly spread, since several church members were in earshot of the outburst. Deacon Frazier leapt across the sanctuary and was on Stanley with a belt in one hand and Stanley's britches in the other before you could sneeze.

After that incident, you couldn't pay Stanley Lee or any other child at New Covenant to give the adults lip service when reprimanded. Ever since that day, the children feared Deacon Frazier. It was well known by everyone at New Covenant that when he had a belt in his hand, he was hell on wheels.

4

The fact that Keith had married Tonya at such a young age weighed heavily on his mind. He was trying to be a man of his word and hang in there for better or worse, but lately the worse was outgrowing the better. Just last week he had to practically beg Tonya to make love to him. Married couples always have problems, but it seemed as if his problems were insurmountable.

Trying to ready himself for the speech he had prepared to give his wife, Keith paced. *Nothing to it but to do it,* he thought. *Let's get this over with."*

As he walked into the room, he noticed his wife sitting under the head dryer with a magazine in her hand. Keith braced himself, preparing to have a blowout with Tonya about her neglect of their marriage.

"We need to talk. I'm tired of being an old married man, Tonya," Keith yelled over the noise of dryer at Tonya, who was flipping through a magazine with pictures of women with spiral curls, pinups, loose curls, and short-cropped hair. He wondered why women bought those magazines in hopes of looking like the models shown. No matter how nice some women's hair turned out, they just weren't going to look like Holly Robinson Peete or or Tyra Banks.

"What?" Tonya yelled back, straining to hear Keith. As he snatched the earplugs of her iPod from her ears, she frowned at him. She wasn't in the mood for his drama.

Keith came closer and yelled louder. "I said I'm tired of being an old married man."

"What are you talking about, K.J?" Tonya asked, as she lifted the hood of the dryer, causing it to turn off.

"You're always doing things for everyone else but me. You make it to all the church functions, choir rehearsals, and prayer meetings, and even visit the sick, but what about me? We've been trying to have a baby for seven and a half years, and you've been too busy to take the time to do even that."

Tonya rolled her eyes at him. "Keith, don't let the devil reign where God rules." This was her favorite saying, and it drove Keith mad every time he heard it. She was beginning to remind him of Sister Peggy, with all her spiritual quotes that no one had ever heard of but her.

"Yeah, yeah, whatever, just know that what one man sees as junk, another sees as treasure." Raising his voice to get his point across, he added, "What you need to do is visit our marriage, because *it's* sick! Rehearse how to be a good wife, and pray about spending time with your husband. I'm tired of eating out and eating food from church events that you bring home."

Slamming the hood of the dryer back down, Tonya rolled her eyes, stuck her earplugs back in her ears, and tuned him out. He had no idea what she was going through, and he never gave her spiritual life any consideration. Now he wanted to cry about home cooking—go figure!

"Keith, I really don't have time for this now. I've got to let my hair dry so it'll look good for tomorrow. Pastor Mitchell is going to be the guest preacher, and you know how he talks about hair being a woman's glory."

Keith glared at Tonya in disbelief. This woman didn't have a clue. He's begging her to hear him out, but she was more interested in what some preacher had to say. He threw his hands in the air and stormed out of the room, leaving Tonya under the hairdryer to continue her attempt at perfection. At that particular moment, he couldn't have cared less about what Pastor Mitchell thought about women's hair; his marriage was falling apart.

Keith left the house, angry and frustrated. He was fed up over the condition of his marriage and Tonya's lack of interest in saving it. He didn't want to end up like his parents, divorced and hating each other, but it certainly looked as if he were heading down that path. If Tonya couldn't see what a jewel he was, he was sure to find a woman who knew a good man when she saw one.

Keith's parents had divorced when he was a high-school senior. They had waited until they felt he was mature enough to deal with the divorce, which they had put on hold since he was twelve years old. His parents had lived in the same house and slept in the same bed but lived two very separate lives. Keith later learned his dad had a girlfriend on the other side of town for many years. His father had visited his girlfriend regularly and openly. He had lost interest in his marriage when his wife had cheated on him and become pregnant with Keith's younger sister, Christine. The marriage was irreparable, but the couple elected to stay together for the children. As soon as Keith was old enough to deal with the reality of his dad not being around, his father split. Keith maintained a close relationship with his dad but had a hard time dealing with the woman his father had married after divorcing his mother.

Tina, his father's new wife, was a petite cinnamon-brown woman, with shoulder-length sandy-brown hair that, she wore in tight curls. She reminded him of Mrs. Ross, his third-grade teacher. Mrs. Ross was very strict and favored her yardstick to keep the class in line. Although Tina was fairly attractive, she wore too much foundation, which gave her complexion a lighter shade and made, her face look artificial. She spent every weekend shopping, which forced his father to get a part-time job to supplement her spending habit.

Tina had very little tolerance for Keith. She doted over her own child but complained whenever Keith vied for his father's attention. Keith's father worked long hours, often going from one job to the next with little sleep, just to make enough money to pay the bills. He often neglected Keith's weekend visits and forgot about Keith's basketball games, or couldn't show up because he was working. Tina refused to give Keith's messages to him and told Keith in no uncertain terms that he wasn't welcome in their home. Keith's father turned a blind eye to Tina's cruelty, which drove a wedge b etween him and his father. Keith stopped visiting their home after he went away to college. If his dad wanted to maintain their relationship, he would have to meet him halfway.

Speeding down the highway toward Shayla Conway's pad, Keith reflected on the changes that had occurred in his marriage over the years. He didn't know how he had been thrown into the arms of another woman; he just knew Tonya wasn't giving him what he needed at home. His infidelity reminded him every day of the failed promise he had made to himself - to never be like his father. Keith thought about what was lacking in his life and saw Shayla as everything that Tonya wasn't—attentive, loving, giving, and understanding. It wasn't that he didn't love his wife; he just didn't feel the same passion as when they'd first gotten married. In the past it had been nothing for him to walk into a room and catch his wife off guard, grab her, and sweep her into his arms. Tonya loved when he'd come home for lunch just to make love in the middle of the day. Now those times were a distant memory.

Keith slowed to a crawl as he spotted a house that reminded him of the home he had shared with his parents as a child, before his father had exited the family dynamic. The two-story wood-framed house with black trim begged to be noticed. Potted flowers hung from the porch's overhang, swaying as the wind pushed past them. A weather-beaten brick chimney leaned with age. The windows were covered, hiding all details of what dwelled behind them. The grass was neatly mowed and the hedged trimmed. The gravel driveway led to the far-right side of the house. At the far-left side was a gorgeous rose bush in full bloom, welcoming the approaching May showers.

The home looked quaint and cozy, but Keith knew from experience that behind closed doors things were never what they appeared from the outside. He reflected on how he had wished for better days in his home when he was growing up. His parents had fought constantly, even after the divorce. He had contemplated running away, but he didn't have anywhere to go.

Wearing only a sheer black negligee, trimmed in lace that tied at the hips, and a pair of six-inch red pumps, Shayla opened the door and greeted him with a wide smile, throwing herself into his arms and embracing him with a deep, wet, passionate kiss. Keith's eyes followed the trail of tiny pink flowers that adorned the material as it led from her bosom to her small waist and stopped at her thighs with a laced-trimmed hem. He grinned as he noticed the red heels, which gave her the extra height to match his tall stature. Shayla grabbed his hand and led him inside. He didn't resist. He knew she'd make him feel like he was the most important man in the world, if only for a short while. Whether or not this was true, he needed the reassurance that he was still a man. Tossing aside his conscience a nd the nagging voice inside him that told him to go home to his wife, Keith closed the door behind him.

5

Keith had met Shayla one evening while he was hanging out with his best friends, Brian and Jerry. He'd found it hard to take his eyes off what he deemed to be the epitome of perfection. Profiling on the hood of a souped-up midnight-blue Mustang was a golden-brown goddess, wearing a pair of very short, revealing denim shorts and a white halter top that showed off her C-cups and left nothing to the imagination. Keith's eyes drifted up and down her body, taking in every curve and estimating her measurements. Her small waist was exposed, revealing the silver ring in her belly button. He also noticed the dip in the base of her spine, which made her backside more pronounced. He gazed at her perfectly trim, long legs; they looked as if they went on forever. She wore sandals that showed off a pair of manicured feet, freshly painted, each toe tipped with a rhinestone. Her sun-kissed loose brown curls bounced around her shoulder blades—a head of hair he knew most women would envy. Keith thought about the line some women used when they wore hair extensions or a weave—"I've got Indian in my family"; he believed this indeed was the case with Shayla. Her high cheekbones and reddish skin tone gave her the appearance of having American Indian descent.

Brian leaned over close to Keith's ear and whispered, 'Don't even think about it. That horse is too wild, and I don't mean the car." The look on Brian's face told Keith his longtime friend was dead serious. Keith looked at the girl again and tried to guess her age. She couldn't have been more than twenty-three. In his eyes anything under twenty was too close to jailbait.

Brian and Keith had been friends since their freshman year of college, when they both had taken an English class from Dr. Whatley. English wasn't Keith's best subject; in fact it kicked his butt. The students called Dr. Thomas

Whatley "Snooze-Button Whatley"—but of course never to his face. Brian had writing and typing skills, which Keith lacked. Dr. Whatley required a ten-page midterm research paper, but Keith simply couldn't produce it. Brian became a big help to him, even going so far as to write his midterm paper for him, which saved him from failing the course and losing his athletic scholarship. He owed Brian his life and often jokingly told him he owed him his firstborn child.

Brian, always the levelheaded friend, had kept Keith out of a lot of sticky situations, but that night nothing he could have said or done would have kept him away from Shayla. Keith thought maybe Brian wanted her for himself, but she was his for the taking.

Keith and Jerry were college roommates who were complete opposites, which is why they got along so well. Jerry was a quiet, average-looking, mild-mannered guy who often went along for the ride. Keith referred to Jerry as his "down-for-whatever cat." Jerry never imposed his opinions on others or preached to Keith like Brian often did. He would only give advice when asked and be done with it; he hated conflict of any sort. When Jerry eyed Shayla, he frowned at her and mumbled under his breath, "Poison!"

Keith looked at him. "Jerry, what's up with you?" First Brian, now Jerry; his friends were coming unglued regarding this girl.

Looking from Shayla to Keith, Jerry answered nonchalantly, "Nothing."

Keith couldn't believe Jerry would speak ill about anyone; it just wasn't like him. "You just called that girl 'poison.' Why?"

Jerry cast his gaze toward the ground as he kicked at a loose piece of concrete on the sidewalk. "She is what she is. Just remember what they say—what goes around comes around. Karma ain't no joke."

Keith was losing patience with Jerry and his riddles. "Man, will you speak English?" he snapped, raising his voice.

Jerry inhaled then blew out a long breath, and looked his friend in the eyes. "That's Shayla, the home wrecker I told you about. She ruined my cousin Rick's marriage a couple of years ago then kicked him to the curb after his wife took the kids, the house, and the money. Never trust a big butt and a smile. It doesn't take a genius to see what she is—poison."

Keith looked at the woman in question and thought about Rick. Too bad Rick couldn't handle his business, but Keith knew that unlike Rick, he was the man! Rick was weak and had gotten caught up in the game. Keith's motto was,

"Players don't get played." He had no kids and a wife who was preoccupied and didn't question his whereabouts; Keith surmised that he was nothing like Rick. Rick, on the other hand, had five kids and a nosy, nagging wife. Keith felt Brian tap his shoulder, which snapped him back to the present.

"A word to the wise, dawg—leave that alone," Brian said. Although Brian could be abrasive with his choice of words, Keith knew his friend always meant well. With that said the three walked on by, leaving Shayla to flirt with other passersby.

Even though Keith had heard what his friends had said, there was something about this girl. He was a grown man who could make his own decisions. He didn't need the guys holding his hand. How could Jerry compare him to his lame cousin Rick— th guy had no game, and according to Jerry, he was scared to talk to women, so how could Keith possibly be in the same category? The more Keith thought about it, the angrier the idea of losing his opportunity with this girl made him. What did Jerry and Brian know about anything anyway?

6

A few weeks after their first encounter, just after leaving work, Keith bumped into the mystery girl he'd seen profiling on the hood of the Mustang. He knew he'd lost the opportunity to meet her while out with his boys, but no one stood in his way now. Keith walked up to her and introduced himself, flashing his million-watt smile her way. He was surprised at how receptive she was to giving him her digits. He grinned, telling himself, *Yep, I still got it!*

Within a couple of weeks, he found himself spending short days and long nights at Shayla's place, forgetting the problems he had with Tonya and her forever-giving heart and full dedication to her first love—New Covenant Full Gospel Church.

Keith knew he couldn't possibly tell Brian or Jerry about his little love affair. *Those guys would lead me straight to the guillotine,* he thought. He couldn't deal with them and the rubbish they spat about this girl; they didn't know her like he did. Shayla was his rock, his shoulder to cry on, and she never bugged him about going to church, because she didn't go to church either. Most Sundays after Tonya left for church, Keith got dressed and left home to spend the day with Shayla. On those Sundays they stayed in bed and shut out the world and its worries. When he was with Shayla, Tonya and her holier-than-thou ways were the furthest thing from his mind, and as he rested in her arms, nothing else mattered. Keith made it a point to beat Tonya home from church, but one particular Sunday, he didn't make it home until very late that night. As he drove home, he knew he'd screwed up, and now he'd have to deal with the consequences. He'd have to concoct a credible story as to why he'd been out all night. He just hated having to deal with the drama. He checked his watch; it was 4:52 a.m.

Trying not to wake his sleeping wife, Keith eased the bedroom door open, gently closed it behind him, and tiptoed into the room.

"Love should have brought you home last night, huh, Keith?" Tonya said, startling him.

"Wha…? Oh, Tonya, You're up? Well, you know how it is when I kick it with the fellows. We lose all track of time. We were just —"Cutting him off midsentence, Tonya yelled, "Save your tired lies for another day. I'm sick of you coming in here smelling like some other woman, booze, cigarettes, and cheap perfume."

"Hold up. You need to slow your roll."

"What you need to do is stay out in those streets with whatever or whoever you're spending money on and your time with!"

"What are you talking about? I was with Brian and Jerry!" Keith raised his voice to drown out Tonya's accusations. *She must have found out about the six hundred dollars I withdrew from our checking account.* Keith couldn't hide the missing money from Tonya. He had helped Shayla pay her rent that month and had planned to put the money back before Tonya got wind of it.

"Do I have 'stupid' written across my forehead? When did you start spending the night with two men?" Tonya stood up and left the bedroom, pausing briefly to throw a dart at Keith. "You're just like your old man!"

"I just told you I was with the guys." Keith felt the dagger that pierced his heart with that last comment but elected to ignore it. Feeling dazed by the attack, he struggled to maintain control of his emotions as he followed her into the hallway.

"Are you gay? Is that it? Are you one of those down-low brothers?" Tonya stared coldly at him, waiting for his reply.

"No! Hell, naw! Give me a break! We just had a few drinks and talked about guy things. You wouldn't understand." Keith knew his story was lame, but he was praying Tonya would bite.

"Make me understand. What's so secretive that you have to share it with the guys and not your wife?" Tonya asked, putting a hand on her hip.

"Give it a rest already!" Keith yelled. "Look, I'm tired and not feeling up to this right now."

He wanted to avoid a fight with Tonya, especially so early in the morning; he was beat. Making love to Shayla twice in an hour had put a dent in his energy.

It was hard keeping up with a woman who was so much younger than him. He decided to let Tonya win this one. Keith looked dejected as he walked toward the bathroom, just wanting to just take a shower then get a little sleep.

He jumped into the shower, trying to scrub off the scent of Shayla. Her fragrance lingered in his nostrils even after he added more liquid soap to his skin. His loofa couldn't scrub away the scratches on his back or the passion marks on his neck. He knew Tonya would find them if she looked at him at the right angle. He quickly washed, dried himself, and slipped into his PJs. He didn't want Tonya to see through his lies with the proof on his body. He braced himself to exit the bathroom, imagining Tonya on the other side of the door with her arms folded and ready to drill him, but when he opened the door, she wasn't there. Feeling relieved, Keith turned off the bedroom light and called it a night.

As he lay awake in bed, he heard Tonya praying in the guest bedroom. Her voice was the familiar soft whine she used only when she prayed. He wondered why people changed their voice when they prayed, as if God only listened when they hummed. He held a pillow over his head, but it still didn't muffle the sound of Tonya pleading to God for mercy, grace, and strength. *"What you need to pray for is love and affection in our marriage and how to pay attention to your husband,* Keith thought.

He felt bold but not so bold to go round for round with Tonya right now. Keith felt guilty about his actions. He hated to see his wife sad; even more than this feeling, he hated the ping in his gut that told him he had done wrong by the woman he had vowed to love. *She brought this on herself,* Keith rationalized, in an attempt to kill the guilt that pricked at his senses. Despite his denial, he knew he also had played a part in creating the stress in his marriage.

Keith finally dozed off, only to be awakened by a thunderous noise. He sat straight up in bed, his heart pumping and breathing halted. Jumping out of bed and sprinting toward the origin of the noise, he grabbed a baseball bat, not necessarily his weapon of choice but accessible.

He ran toward the front of the house, bat in hand, but his panic subsided when he saw Tonya pacing the floor with a Bible in one hand and blessed oil in the other, casting out demons and telling them to be bound and to return to the pits of hell in the name of Jesus. Keith's mouth flew open in amazement.

He'd come flying through the house thinking they were being burglarized, only to find his wife at war with unseen entities.

Satisfied that a burglary wasn't being committed, he angrily turned on his heels and headed back to bed, shaking his head and mumbling, "That woman has finally flipped her wig."

Unable to sleep, Keith tossed and turned as his rambling thoughts took over his psyche. His thoughts raced as the metamorphosis of his marriage danced before him. *What happened to the love and laughter we once had?* he wondered. He couldn't pinpoint the exact moment his marriage had taken a turn for the worse. He reflected on better days, when he and Tonya had been best friends, a time when they had been one, a time when no one could come between them. He knew she was his soul mate, but he couldn't stop himself from marring his marriage with his indiscretions.

Keith's problems seemed to dissipate as sleep found him and sent him to a cloud where he discovered memories of a better time, when life with Tonya was nothing short of heaven.

Tonya had put up with the phone calls that ended with the caller hanging up when she answered the phone. It was funny how many "wrong numbers" Keith received late at night when he answered. Two o'clock calls that woke her out of her sleep had led to brief mumbles into the phone as he spoke to the caller then hung up with the same lie—"Wrong number."

There was nothing wrong with her mind or senses. She'd always been told that if it looked, walked, or talked like a duck, it was definitely a duck.

Too often she had tried to convince Keith to attend church with her, to be an attentive husband, and to spend less time with his friends. His complaints about her spending less time at home only mirrored her complaints concerning him.

7

At five o'clock the following Sunday morning, a sharp pain in Tonya's lower abdomen snatched her from her slumber. She felt as if her insides were being pulled apart and twisted like a pretzel. At breakneck speed she launched from the bed and raced to the bathroom, stubbing her big toe on the bottom of the bedpost. Pushing past the pain that radiated throughout her foot, she made it to the commode in the nick of time. As she knelt on the floor in agony, waiting for the next tidal wave of nausea to take over her body, Keith entered the bathroom.

Leaning against the doorframe with a concerned expression, he asked, "Are you all right? You catapulted out of bed like the house was on fire."

Looking pitiful and feeling weak and helpless, Tonya whined, "What was in that lasagna you cooked last night? I'm sick as a dog."

"Nothing different than when I made it the last twenty times It never made you sick before, so don't blame this on my cooking."

"I don't know what it is, but something made me sick. Maybe it…" Before she could finish her statement, nausea again swept over her. Grabbing the porcelain base, she expelled what seemed to be the remainder of her stomach's contents.

After half an hour of dry heaving, the feeling of nausea had passed. The room continued to spin as Tonya staggered back to bed. Her stomach felt as if she had pulled a muscle, and her chest wall ached from her having leaned over the toilet for so long. She prayed she hadn't contracted some deadly illness like E coli or mad cow disease.

Keith returned from the bathroom with a cool, damp washcloth and placed it on his wife's forehead. Climbing into bed beside Tonya, he wondered whether she still planned to go to church or whether she had the guts to stay home for just one day.

As if she'd read his mind, Tonya panted, "I sure hate not being able to hear Pastor Mullin's sermon this morning. I guess I should call Sister Peggy and tell her I won't be able to make it."

Irritated by her comment, Keith rolled his eyes then hastily turned over in bed in an attempt to go back to sleep. He couldn't care less what Pastor Mullin or Sister Peggy thought; he had stopped attending New Covenant Full Gospel about six years ago. In his opinion, Tonya went to church enough for the both of them.

Tonya continued to feel sick later that morning, and since she had nothing left to bring up, the dry heaves were just as bad. She knew she wouldn't be able to go to church today or to work on Monday, she needed to be seen by her doctor, and soon.

After she regained her bearings, she climbed out of bed, grabbed the telephone book, and attempted to look up her doctor's number *Why can't I remember his number when I need it?* she thought. She needed an immediate appointment—like yesterday.

The woman who answered the phone informed Tonya that the earliest appointment would be in three days. *I could be dead by then,* Tonya thought but reluctantly accepted the appointment. Realizing she had been going nonstop over the past three weeks trying to plan and prepare for Pastor Mullin's visit to New Covenant's upcoming conference, she felt rundown; maybe she just needed a boost of vitamins. She had helped with the hotel reservations for his church members, assisted in planning the menu for the after-service brunch, and also helped organize the women's symposium, which was taking place on Saturday, before the main service. Maybe she had simply worn down her body. Her dad had warned her about trying to be a one-woman show, but it never seemed as if things went right unless she did them herself.

8

As Tonya entered the waiting room of Dr. Gipson's office, she didn't feel any better. Her insides seemed to be doing somersaults, and nothing stayed in her stomach. Surmising her illness was due to food poisoning, she made , a mental note never to eat Keith's cooking again.

"Hi, my name's Tonya Paris. I have an appointment for nine o'clock with Dr. Gipson." Forcing herself to smile at the woman who gave little thought as to who she was and why she was even there, she waited for the receptionist to return her smile. She simply pointed at the appointment book then told Tonya to sign in and have a seat. Reluctantly Tonya left the receptionist window and took a seat as instructed. She had a mind to give the woman a verbal lashing for being so rude, but she felt sicker than a three-legged dog, as Sister Peggy would say.

In the seating area, a TV mounted on the wall was showing a medical program that promoted breast-feeding over bottle-feeding. Magazines on parenting, healthy eating, and immunizations were displayed on the table, and along the wall in a rack. Deciding to read a parenting magazine that featured a smiling baby and a beaming mother, Tonya stood to retrieve the reading material to pass the time.

As she crossed the room to the magazine rack, the door next to the receptionist desk opened. A round-faced, brown-skinned nurse, with deep dimples that appeared when she smiled, came through the door that led to the exam rooms.

"Tonya Paris!" she announced, as if Tonya would win a prize if she answered correctly.

"I'm Tonya Paris," she replied, placing the magazine back in the rack and walking to the open door.

"Dr. Gipson will be with you shortly, Mrs. Paris, but in the meantime, please follow me. I'll take your vital signs and height and weight, and we'll also need to collect a urine sample."

Tonya followed the nurse, whose nametag read, "Glenda Brown, RN," to get her vitals taken. Her blood pressure was elevated, but she'd expected it would be, because she'd had a terrible headache since Sunday morning. After her height and weight were taken, she proceeded down the narrow hallway to the bathroom with a specimen cup in hand.

Why do they always ask you to pee in a cup after you've already used the bathroom? Tonya wondered, as she strained to get the last drop of urine out, missing the cup entirely.

She smiled as she handed the urine sample to the nurse. "I hope this is enough," she said. "It's hard to aim at that little cup."

Taking the cup in her gloved hand, Nurse Brown smiled. "This should be plenty. Thank you." She led Tonya to an exam room, where she took a brief medical history from her then gave her a blue paper gown. The nurse asked her to remove all her clothing and to put on the gown. Dr. Gipson would be with her shortly. With that the nurse left the room, leaving her to wait.

Tonya undressed, slipped on the thin blue gown, and sat on the cold exam table to wait for the doctor. The paper made a loud crinkly noise against the exam table every time she moved, which annoyed her. She became more anxious as she waited, thinking, *Why do they always put you in a cold room, half naked, and make you wait half an hour before you see the doctor? And when are they going to invent a gown that covers your rear end?*

After what seemed an eternity, Tonya heard a light knock on the door as Dr. Gipson walked into the room. Speaking in a soft tone that made him seem very professional, he gently shook Tonya's hand. "Hi, Mrs. Paris. What brings you in today?" Tonya looked into the face of the handsome thirty-something, clean-shaven hazel-eyed doctor. His eyes didn't seem to match his chocolate complexion. Tonya wondered whether he wore colored contact lenses. "I think I have food poisoning," she told him, "because Sunday I woke up feeling like death warmed over."

Tonya pondered the idea of actually dying from food poisoning. What would her family do without her? How could her father go on after losing both a wife and a daughter? She pushed the thought out of her mind and rebuked the Devil for putting such a morbid thought in her head.

Interrupting Tonya thoughts, Dr. Gipson said, "Well, let's make sure you haven't picked up any bugs. I'd like to get some blood work on you as well."

The doctor finished his examination and prescribed something for her upset stomach. She felt better just having seen him, even though she didn't have a clue as to what was wrong with her. She made a follow-up appointment with the receptionist before leaving the office. Then she made a run to the pharmacy before heading home to climb into bed.

9

Tonya had little patience for Mary and her intrusiveness this morning. Nothing stopped her from prying into other people's affairs, so why would this morning be any different?

Snatching her head up with a jerk, Mary eyed Tonya. "You must have partied too much last night, because you look like a hangover gone wrong!" she said with a chuckle.

Tonya frowned at her, pursed her lips, and threw her hands in the air. She wasn't worth a retort. Tonya continued toward her office. She didn't feel much better than she had the day before, but she didn't want to stay home another day. After taking the medication for her upset stomach, she felt much better, but her head was still hurting. She'd get her blood pressure rechecked when she went back to Dr. Gipson's office for her follow-up appointment that afternoon.

Tonya took her time driving to the doctor's office. She hated going to the doctor, but she especially hated going to Dr. Gipson's office and dealing with the nasty receptionist. The woman's dull, unconcerned eyes and mannerisms always made the visit uncomfortable. She reminded Tonya of the woman in the 1970s movie *Car Wash* who sat behind the desk painting her nails and trying to look pretty all day while neglecting her work. Tonya's dad always said, "If you don't do your job with excellence, someone else might be waiting to do it for you."

Reluctantly Tonya entered the doctor's office for her follow-up exam. She went through the routine of sitting and waiting to be called by the nurse. When her blood pressure was taken, Tonya noticed it was no longer elevated, which was good news.

Dr. Gipson shook her hand and looked at her with a gleam in his eyes. "I got your results back from your urine specimen. Your hCG is positive."

Tonya lifted her right hand to interrupt him. "My…what is positive?" she stammered.

Dr. Gipson quickly explained himself. "Your pregnancy test came back positive."

Feeling confused, Tonya could only muster an "Oh."

"Is this good news, Mrs. Paris?" Dr. Gipson asked, while looking down at his clipboard.

Tonya managed a weak smile. "Of course. We've been trying for a while, so I guess that explains why I can't keep anything down." She felt better knowing why she was sick, but she couldn't wrap her mind around the idea of being pregnant. Tonya's insides began to heat up; her heart skipped beats; and she had forgotten how to breathe. She couldn't wait to tell Keith the news. After all this time, they finally were going to have the child they wanted so much. Tonya wondered what this news would mean to Keith. She hopped it would bring them closer, because lately she was starting to feel like they were total strangers. Tonya wasn't one who believed a baby could keep a man, but it did change situations. She knew those changes weren't always for the better, but all she could do was keep praying. Trying to hype herself up about the pregnancy, Tonya belted out, "Hallelujah! God has answered my prayers!" The thought of being a mother changed her view of her marriage and her future with Keith. She now felt her marriage was worth fighting for, and she praised God for her good news. A child would bring character to the family and peace of mind to her husband, who was beginning to believe he couldn't have children. It was hard to believe that in eight months they would be parents.

Halfway home from the doctor's office, Tonya called Keith to tell him she needed to talk to him. His secretary, Angela, a middle-aged white woman who had started working with Keith three years ago, told Tonya he wasn't available for phone calls at the time. Tonya became anxious, which sent her mind spiraling in a million directions. *Why can't he take a phone call? Is he having an affair with some tramp at work? Is it Angela, his precious secretary?*

Angela's voice broke through Tonya's irrational thoughts. "Would you like to leave a message? He should be out of his meeting in about an hour."

Feeling ashamed, Tonya neglected to leave a message or say good-bye; instead she closed her flip phone and shook her head.

How did I get to this point? she wondered. *What's wrong with me?*

The ringing phone startled Tonya, as she sat contemplating the future of her family.

"Hey, girl. What happened to you on Sunday?"

Tonya recognized Carmen's voice. The two sisters always had been closer than most sisters, especially since their mother had died when they were young.

"I thought I was a goner when I woke up Sunday. I have a really bad stomachache. I thought my body would literally turn inside out before I got some relief!"

"Well, I just wanted to let you know you missed a treat!" Carmen always gave Tonya the 411 on church gossip. "Sister Peggy, Mother Poole, and Sister Hattie turned that church out!" Tonya heard Carmen trying to muffle her laugh as she attempted to relive the performance of the trio. "While the choir was singing, Sister Peggy got the Holy Ghost and started yelling 'Jesus! Kick me through the goal poles one more time!' As she was about to dive face-first into the floor, Sister Hattie shook and screamed real loud and spoke in tongues over Sister Peggy's jerking body on the floor." Carmen choked on her laughter. Tonya visualized tears streaming down her sister's cheeks as she laughed while recapping Sunday's service. Carmen always shed tears when she laughed; it was an automatic response.

Tonya tried to imagine the scene the women must have caused on this special Sunday morning. Whenever a guest preacher and his church members visited, the trio always attempted to outdo one another during praise service.

As Carmen tried to regain her composure, she gasped for air to keep from howling all over again. "Girl, the worst part was that while this was going on, Mother Poole felt the spirit and started dancing around the church, not watching where she was going, and collided into Sister Hattie."

Tonya was hoping the women were OK, but Carmen was laughing so hard that she couldn't ask her.

"Mother Poole went one way, and her teeth went the other! Sister Hattie's blond wig flew off her head as she landed upside down on top of Sister Peggy.

Girl, the choir had to stop singing just to get the women back into their seats." Carmen was in hysterics over the whole fiasco.

After Carmen calmed herself, Tonya took the opportunity to tell her the news she had received from Dr. Gipson. She was unsure how Keith would take it, but she knew Carmen would be elated.

"Get out!" Carmen screamed.

Tonya snatched the phone away from her ear. As she did, she still could hear Carmen laughing and repeating, "No way!" Tonya smiled at her sister's excitement.

Carmen sang, "I'm gonna be an aunt! I'm gonna be an aunt." By the sound of the rustling of the telephone, Tonya knew her sister was dancing around. That girl would make a song out of anything.

"Just wait until I tell Daddy." Tonya knew Elder Lacey would be excited about his first grandchild. "And Carmen, let me tell him, you bigmouth."

Filled with excitement Tonya rehearsed in her mind how she would tell Keith the good news. How would he take it? "Nothing to it, but to do it!" Dialing the number that she'd dialed so many times before, she took a deep breath as she to be transferred to Keith's direct line.

"Hello?" He answered in his deep voice that was reserved for business.

She opened her mouth to speak, but nothing came out. She rubbed her forehead in frustration. *Get it together Tonya*, she told herself.

"Hello?" he repeated with a hint of irritation. He was busy and every minute counted.

"Keith, I've got gotten from my doctor's visit." Tonya's stomach began to tighten as she coached herself to open the door for acceptance or rejection.

"Is everything alright?" His voice became a whisper as it filled with concern.

"Yes, everything is just fine. In fact, you're going to be a father."

Silence.

"Keith did you hear me?" Tonya heart began to race. She didn't expect this reaction.

"um, yes, I did." His voice was cracking as she spoke into the receiver.

"Are you happy?"

"I am ecstatic!"

Tonya could hear the change in his voice. He was clearly moved by the news. She breathed a sigh of relief after realizing that Keith was as accepting of the pregnancy as she.

"I guess we have something to celebrate."

Tonya could hear the laughter in Keith's voice.

I'll prepare you favor meal."

"Not tonight, dinner's on me. I'll make dinner reservations for seven"

Now all she had to do was get to her father before Carmen blabbed.

10

Keith didn't know how to feel about the news of a baby after all this time; he felt torn.H He had to choose between leaving his wife, which he had promised Shayla, or staying and being a father to his child and working on his marriage. He'd wanted a child from day one of his marriage. What kind of father would he be living the life he'd created? He couldn't simply walk away from his marriage now, not when things were just beginning to turn around for them. Keith also knew he couldn't leave Shayla; he had developed strong feelings for her. Shayla was his shining star, his emotional connection, the youth he clung to, and his fantasy fulfilled. He thought about the first time he and Shayla had made love; it was an eye-opening experience. Shayla did things with her body that he thought should be illegal. She also played with his mind and toyed with his emotions, but he wasn't willing to walk away. Tonya, on the other hand, made him feel as if making love to him was a chore she had to perform because it was a wifely duty. Despite his personal feelings toward Tonya, he knew his place was with his wife, for better or worse.

Shayla wrapped her arms around Keith's neck and kissed him deeply, pulling him inside as he stood in her doorway; she knew how to make him weak. He tasted her fruit-flavored lip gloss, smelled the sweet fragrance of her perfume, and felt the soft flesh he held in his hands. He had lost all control of his senses, forgetting the reason for his visit. Shaking his head to clear his thoughts, he took a step back, putting space between him and Shayla; he had to think. How could he tell the woman he had so much passion for that it was over? He could no longer hurt his wife; he needed to concentrate on his marriage. Seeing Keith's slight resistance, Shayla grabbed him and kissed him once more. Keith removed her arms from his neck and headed to the couch. As he sat down, he asked her to join him. He knew she wouldn't take the news well, but he'd deal with that later. Knowing all hell was about to break loose, he finally told her what was on his mind.

"Shayla, I can't leave my wife now. What kind of husband would I be?" he tried to explain to her, after telling her he and Tonya were expecting a baby.

Shayla barricaded her body in front of the doorway with one hand on her hip. "You ain't no kind of husband, because you laid up here with me every night!"

I don't need this drama, Keith thought. He couldn't understand why Shayla couldn't just let things go; he could never have a life with her. Besides, you don't marry strippers, hookers, or groupies, and Shayla was all of the above. She'd do anything for a buck, and twice as much for two.

"What about me? What about us?" Shayla asked, following Keith to the door. She wedged her body between him and the door to prevent his departure.

"Look, I made a mistake, and you got caught in the middle, and for that I'm sorry, but I have a family at home that needs me."

Keith pushed past her, ending this secret life, to return home to be the faithful husband his wife deserved.

"Every dog's got his day, and your day's coming!" Shayla stood in the door-way yelling as he walked away.

Keith hopped into his car, leaving his sin behind him. Shayla was a mistake he had made; now he had to focus on his marriage.

He had regrets about Shayla. He knew she hadn't been faithful to him, but how could he ask that of her when he was a married man himself? Her son's father was locked up again for breaking the law. He was what they call a repeat offender, spending more time on the inside than as a free man. Rumor had it that he had a lover on the inside, which is what kept him going back to prison. Whenever he was released from prison, Shayla made it a point to give him a place to live and anything else on the menu.

A few months after Keith had gotten together with Shayla, he and Brian had gone out cruising one night. Brian had told him he had something to show him. Keith's mind began to wander. *What could possibly be so important that Brian would keep a secret from me?* As the two men got closer to the familiar neigh-borhood, Keith knew something was up. Brian slowed down and quietly let Keith put the pieces together. Shayla's son's father, Eric Thomas, known on the streets as "Big E," had parked his car in her driveway. The car was probably stolen—how else could he afford a brand-new Lexus coupe after getting out of prison? That explained why Shayla suddenly had wanted some space in their relationship and had asked him to call before coming over. Everyone knew that when Big E wa s out of prison his home was with her. Keith nodded to Brian, and they quietly drove away. Even after Brian had shown him the truth, Keith went right back to Shayla after Big E had gotten locked up. He was arrested after being fingered as the triggerman when a man had been shot over a sour drug deal.

Now with the family he always had wanted finally happening, Keith had to focus on his new beginning and get his life back on track. Tonya was happy about their expected newcomer and spent less time running around and trying to be the entire sisterhood auxiliary of New Covenant and paid more attention to their home life. Keith just wished the newcomer had come much sooner; perhaps his marriage would be a lot healthier.

Sitting in his car outside of his office building, Keith pulled out his cell phone and dialed Brian's number. "I wish I'd never met that chick. She's straight crazy!" he told him.

"You never listen until it's too late. Jerry and I warned you about her time and time again. She's bad news."

"Kick a man when he's down, why don't you?"

"I hate to be the one to say, 'I told you so,' but I told you so!" Brian said sarcastically. He knew how to get under Keith's skin.

"Hindsight is twenty-twenty, so drilling me about this does very little for me right now."

"It wouldn't be hindsight if you'd listen for once in your life."

"My mom always said I was hardheaded as a kid," Keith joked, but his laugh was hollow and lifeless. He was really kicking himself for not listening to his friends.

"Yeah? Well, my mom always said that a hard head makes for a soft behind."

"True, but what can I say? I messed up."

"Why her, K.J.? You didn't really believe you could have something with a girl like that, did you?"

"I guess I was just caught up."

"I just hope Tonya is understanding about all of this."

"What do you mean, 'understanding'? Man, I can't tell my wife about this!"

"Believe me, she already knows. They always know."

"So what do I do now?" Keith asked, suddenly feeling nervous about facing Tonya.

"K.J., go home, man. Go home and face the music," Brian said, before hanging up the phone. He never ended a call with a good-bye or any clue that he was about to hang up. You knew he was gone when you heard the dial tone. Although Jerry and Keith had brought this to his attention at least several times a week, he still refused to end his calls with a proper good-bye.

Looking at the phone and shaking his head, Keith placed his cell phone back in its holder and headed home. "Dude, learn some phone etiquette!" he said out loud.

11

Tonya heard the loud shrill of the phone repeatedly before she could get the key out of the lock. She dropped her bag to the ground. "Lord, there go my eggs!" She sighed deeply as she noticed the wet stain forming on the brown paper bag that held her groceries. She raced to the phone and reached it on the last ring. "Hello?" she panted into the receiver.

"Mrs. Paris?" the voice on the other end asked with uncertainty.

"Yes, this is Mrs. Paris. How may I help you?" Tonya said, annoyed at having to rush to the phone for some telemarketer. *Are they going to replace my eggs if I buy a magazine or a satellite dish?*

"This is Nurse Brown, from Dr. Gipson's office. We'd like to set up an appointment to speak with you about your lab results."

"Well, can't you talk to me now? I'm already on the phone."

There was a pause before the nurse continued. "I'm sorry, Mrs. Paris, but Dr. Gipson needs to discuss your test results with you in person. We'd like you to come to the office as soon as you can. Is tomorrow good for you?"

Puzzled, Tonya looked at the phone. What could be so serious about her test results that the nurse couldn't tell her? A frown crossed her face as she tried to figure out what the secrecy was all about. They already had told her she was pregnant. Now what?

"Sure, I can come on my lunch break, if that's all right."

"Good. I'll put you down for noon. We look forward to seeing you then."

After hanging up the phone, Tonya went back to her bag of groceries to inspect the damage, hoping most of her eggs had survived.

The next day she spent the entire morning wondering what Dr. Gipson had found in her labs that could possibly be so important and urgent. Watching the clock didn't make the hours go by any faster, and the office noise made her feel even more anxious. The ringing phone kept her on edge, and her coworkers were just as annoying, because they wanted to talk to her. Tonya knew it was just her being on edge that made every little thing seem magnified. She needed a cigarette break, even though she didn't smoke. The thought of having to take a cigarette break made her wonder what kind of break nonsmokers took. Her high level of anxiety was beginning to make her feel and think as if she were high on some type of herb. *Marijuana makes you think about things no one else wonders about*, she thought. Yep, she definitely needed a break. She decided to take an early lunch.

She elected to drive over Dr. Gipson's office early to get her lab results and put her mind at ease. Checking her watch, she calculated how much time she'd have before her lunch break was over. Thirty minutes at Dr. Gipson's office should leave her with just enough time to grab something quick to eat and get back to the office before the end of her lunch break.

Walking past Mary's desk, Tonya rolled her eyes. Mary was too busy in her phone chatter to even notice her leaving. The woman was cackling so much that her wig was bobbing and slipping around her head with a rhythm of its own.

As Tonya entered the doctor's office, she noticed it wasn't as crowded as it had been the last time she was there, but the receptionist was just as unfriendly.

What does it cost to get a smile around here? she thought, as she approached the window.

"Mrs. Paris," the receptionist said, "Dr. Gipson will be with you shortly."

Taking a seat in a chair facing the TV screen, she prepared to wait. She noticed a young couple in the corner sitting quietly and holding hands. The woman looked to be all of eight months' pregnant, and the man appeared to be carrying the pregnancy himself around his midsection. *It must be their first child,* Tonya thought.

Nurse Brown interrupted her thoughts as she called Tonya's name. "Mrs. Paris, the doctor will see you now." As she was led to the exam room to wait for Dr. Gipson, she thought, *Strip to blue and chill 'til the doctor arrives*, referring to the blue paper gown, the cold exam room, and the long wait she'd experienced on her last visit. Since she was there just to get her test results, she was spared the routine of getting undressed. To pass the time as she waited for Dr. Gipson, she took out the book she was reading, which was about how to get along with difficult people. She needed it to deal with those clowns she worked with.

Startled by the knock on the door, Tonya jumped as she looked up to see Dr. Gipson's smiling face peering around the door.

"Hello, Mrs. Paris. How are you today?" the doctor asked, extending his hand.

Shaking his hand, Tonya tried to perk up, but her stomach was doing flips, and her nerves were getting the best of her. "Hi. I guess I'm OK. I've been experiencing a little morning sickness, but I guess that's to be expected."

Dr. Gipson bit his bottom lip and furrowed his brow as he braced himself. He looked as if he were having a difficult time getting his word out; in fact he looked more nervous than she did.

"Mrs. Paris, I called you in to talk about the lab tests results from the sample we drew on your initial visit. I requested a series of labs to rule out any infections that could be harmful to the fetus, one of which was an HIV test. It's a standard test we do on all our expected mothers, with your consent of course."

If this is such a standard test, why does he seem so nervous? Tonya thought.

"I received your results and was very concerned when they came back positive."

Tonya looked confused. "Positive is good, isn't it?"

Dr. Gipson took her hands in his. "Mrs. Paris, normally positive is good but not when it comes to this test. If you'd like..."

Tonya could see the doctor's lips moving, but she could no longer hear the words that were flowing from his mouth. She knew what HIV meant, but why was he telling her this? Why was he saying she had something as ridiculous as HIV? *He has to be mistaken*, she thought. *Those tests aren't onehundredpercent accurate.* Suddenly Dr. Gipson began to fade away, and the room grew dark and still.

"Mrs. Paris, can you hear me? Mrs. Paris?"

Tonya heard several people calling her name. It sounded like they were in a tunnel, and she couldn't focus to see who was calling her. *Is this some sort of dream, or maybe a horrific nightmare?* Her head felt like someone had hit her with a sledgehammer. As light made its way behind her eyelids, Tonya slowly opened her eyes. She could make out Dr. Gipson, Nurse Brown, and an unfamiliar woman standing over her.

No. It's definitely not a dream. "What happened?" she asked, after realizing she was sprawled out on the floor and the voices she'd heard were these people standing over her. She also realized the light was a penlight that Dr. Gipson was holding over her eyes.

Dr. Gipson's voice sounded strained. "Mrs. Paris, are you OK? You fell off the exam table and hit your head on the floor. I'd like to send you to see Dr. Freeman to get an X-ray and perhaps an MRI and an ultrasound to make sure you didn't injure yourself or the baby."

After lifting an unsteady Tonya off the floor, the three braced her as she struggled to find her sense of balance. She couldn't stand on her own, which was a sign of something being wrong, but what? As Tonya focused on the young lady whom she didn't recognize, she read her nametag, "Linda Byrd, LPN."

Dr. Gipson noticed Tonya's dazed and puzzled expression. "Mrs. Paris, this is Linda. She'll escort you to Dr. Freeman's office for your tests. Is there anyone you can call to drive you home? You're not in any shape to drive yourself."

Tonya's mind began to spin out of control. *Dr. Freeman? Xrays? Escort? What's going on? Why is my head hurting so badly?* She opened her mouth to speak, but no words formed. Tears slid down her face. *HIV positive? How?*

12

The time between being transported to Dr. Freeman's office to being driven home by Carmen was a total blur. Tonya remembered giving the nurse Carmen's cellphone number and her sister meeting her at the radiology clinic, but rest of the day escaped her, as she tried to wrap her mind around this newfound knowledge. Rubbing her forehead, she tried to clear the fog that surrounded her mind. Tonya felt the constant pulsating pain in her head from the fall she had taken earlier in Dr. Gipson's exam room. She was in desperate need of an aspirin. Looking in her medicine cabinet, she remembered Sister Peggy telling her that Tylenol was much safer for the baby. When she reached for the Tylenol, she felt a sharp pain in her back. "Aw!" she screamed, as she jerked her arm back to her side. Grabbing the bottle of pills, she decided to ignore her onelimit rule and settled on two. She downed the pills with a glass of tap water. *I guess the Tylenol will have to work for both this headache and my aching back*, she thought. *I must have taken one heck of a dive off that table.*

Not being able to remember half of what had happened to her that day left her bewildered. Tonya slowly made her way to her bedroom to rest, each step making her feel as if the blood vessels in her head would burst. She sprawled across the bed, hoping against all hope that somewhere someone had made a huge mistake and trying to convince herself that there was a silver lining, *Maybe things will be clearer in the morning*, she thought.

Carmen insisted on staying with her, but Tonya asked that she leave so she could get some sleep. She was finally able to persuade her sister to leave by telling her that Keith would be home soon.

Carmen had left more than an hour ago; at this moment Tonya wished she had her sister at her side. She began to panic about the whole ordeal and didn't know how she'd break the news to her sister or Keith that she was sick. She knew the news would kill her father; he'd already lost so much. *It's easy to give good news,* Tonya thought, *but it seems an impossible task to give news of this caliber to people you love. How will they take it?*

—⁂—

She reached over to slap the snooze button on the alarm clock. It was five o'clock in the morning, her usual time to get up and get her day started, and it was still dark outside. After a few minutes, she reluctantly got out of bed. "I feel like a drunk with a hangover that lasted for days," Tonya mumbled. Looking behind her, she saw that Keith was still sound asleep and wondered what time he'd come home last night. The sudden details of yesterday's event came back to her in a flash—*HIV positive.* Tonya immediately felt queasy and rushed to the bathroom to throw up, but since she hadn't eaten in the last twenty-four hours, she had nothing to bring up, which made her feel even worse. After slamming down the commode lid, she sat down with a thud and reflected on the terrible news.

I've never had a blood transplant and never got stuck with a dirty needle, and I've only been with my husband sexually. How can this be? It's got to be a mistake. I'll call Dr. Gipson as soon as the office opens and get him to retest me. Surely it's a mistake. I'm sure my blood work got swapped with someone else's. Yeah, that's it. They probably had the wrong patient chart; people make mistakes all the time. Making a mental note to call Dr. Gipson's office when she got to work, Tonya jumped in the shower. *I'd better get ready,* she thought. *Bills don't pay themselves.*

—⁂—

As Tonya arrived to work and prepared for a long day of paper pushing, ringing phones, and nerve-wracking coworkers, she spotted Mary standing in the hall-way talking with Rhonda, another coworker she didn't particularly like. Mary waved at her in an attempt to get her attention, and reluctantly Tonya slowed her pace. One thing Tonya hated more than gossiping women was loud gos-siping women.

Mary was in her midfifties but thought she was still in her twenties. She wore a bright-red wig, loads of makeup, and three coats of mascara around her coal-black eyes. Her feet always fell over her shoes like muffin tops, and she wore clothes that were at least two sizes too small. She claimed she was a size fourteen, when it was clear to anyone looking at her bulges that she was easily a size twenty-two. Mary blamed her weight on having a baby. Well, that would be legit if she'd just had the baby, but Mary's baby was thirty-two years old and certainly couldn't be blamed for her weight problem. Push the plate away once in a while and she might just lose a pound or two.

"Hey, Tonya," Mary said. "Hope you're feeling better, since you didn't come back after lunch yesterday." She was so loud that everyone in the office could hear her. As Mary got closer to Tonya, her smile dropped as she zoomed in on Tonya's puffy eyes. Tonya's face couldn't hide the truth; her eyes were those of a person who'd been crying not to mention the golf ball size hematoma on her forehead. "Girl, are you OK? You look like hell!"

Tonya flinched at Mary's description. Then she noticed other coworkers stopping what they were doing to glance in her direction. Mary was both loud and ignorant. The word *discreet* never had been in her vocabulary. Tonya was sure everyone in the office had heard her.

"Thanks, Mary. Now I feel *much* better."

"Sorry. I didn't mean to hurt your feelings. Is there anything you'd like to talk about? I think you should go home. I heard about your accident yesterday. AAre you all right?"

There's certainly some truth to the saying that Mary's nose is in everybody's business. She's been known to eavesdrop on the office phone lines. Tonya knew that there was no other way Mary could have known about her accident. She was the tap line to the well of the office gossip.

Shifting her weight from one foot to the other, Tonya considered the offer but thought better of it and decided she needed the distraction of work to take her mind off her troubles.

"Thanks Mary, but I think I'll stay. I need the hours, especially with the baby coming."

Mary gave her a brisk hug and again offered a listening ear if she needed to talk.

"I'm fine. I just need to get my day started." Tonya thanked her for her offer but again said no. Feeling embarrassed by Mary's fake display of concern, she headed to her office.

Tonya hurriedly closed her office door, plopped down at her desk, and cried. Mary's insensitivity deeply penetrated her heart. She already vulnerable; she didn't need Mary's added insult. Mary was as fake as the gaudy cheapjewelryshe wore. It was no mystery in the office that if there was anything you didn't want to get out, you shouldn't let Mary know, because she wasn't one to keep a secret. Tonya knew that one word of her problem to Mary and the entire office would learn of her condition. She reminded Tonya of one of her church members, Sister Lillie White. Sister White knew everybody's business and couldn't keep her mouth shut to save her own life. If Sister White were drowning and had the choice of keeping her mouth closed in order to live or tell the latest gossip and drown, she'd tell whatever gossip she'd heard as she took her last breath.

Sister White never came right out and started gossiping; she was too clever for that. She'd always start off with an opening such as, "Sister, I need for you to pray!" or "Sister, when you go into your prayer closet, remember Sister soandso." All the while her main motive was to spread some poor unsuspecting church member's business. Sister White was known to cause confusion and discord in the church, but when the pastor based his sermon on the subject, she'd be the loudest one in church, yelling "Amen! Preach the word, man of God!"

What the man of God needed to do was to wag his finger in Sister White's face—better yet, sit on her lap and preach his sermon. Maybe then she'd get the picture that he was talking to her and not just everyone else. But no matter how hard Pastor Mullin preached about gossiping women in the church, she never felt he was stepping on her toes.

When her son Patrick had come out as both gay and transgender and asked to be called "Patricia, Sister White was beside herself. She didn't pick up the phone and tell anyone about that he wore women's clothes on the weekend and had even started wearing her shoes when he was sixteen. One Sunday Patrick showed up to church as Patricia, wearing a shoulderlength platinumblond weave in his hair, a pair of red pumps, and a ladies' white pantsuit set off with a redandwhite scarf around his neck. Sister White was mortified w hen he walked into the sanctuary. She must have sat through the whole service without hearing a word the pastor said, because she didn't utter a single Amen that morning. The look on her face said she'd rather be buried six feet deep than be at New Covenant Full Gospel at that moment.

While his mother sat there feeling mortified, Patrick saw it as his finest moment. He was proud to be Patricia and refused to answer to his birth name. The funny thing about people who like to gossip is that it's only fun when the gossip is about someone else.

13

As Tonya got dressed, she hummed her favorite song by BeBe and CeCe Winans, "I'm Lost without You." She was very excited about getting her ultrasound done today; she'd finally get to see her little one. If everything went well, she'd soon know the sex of her baby. The only thing she didn't like about the test was being forced to drink four glasses of water, which felt like a gallon to her. The worst part was not being able to go to the bathroom. How did they expect her to hold that much water? Didn't they know that pregnant women have to pee at least fifty times a day?

Keith busied himself in the bathroom, showering and shaving. She heard him bustling around in his haste. He acted as if he were getting ready for the prom. That man spent more time in front of a mirror than a teenage girl. Tonya tapped on the door. "Let's get a move on, K.J.!" she called out. She didn't want to be late for her appointment.

Keith emerged from the bathroom brimming with enthusiasm. He cupped Tonya's face with his hands. "A thing of beauty is a joy forever," he said, then kissed her forehead.

Tonya hadn't seen this side of Keith in such a long time. It was so refreshing.

As she climbed into her husband's car, she felt like she had gained twenty pounds from the water alone.

"Come on, slowpoke!" Keith teased her, as she eased into the passenger seat.

"If I move too fast I won't be able to hold this water."

"Do I need to cover the seat with towels?"

"Very funny!" Tonya said.

Just then her cell phone rang. She grabbed her purse and retrieved her phone. Checking the caller ID, she saw Carmen's name displayed on the screen.

"Hey, girl. What's up?" Carmen asked, as soon as Tonya flipped open her cell.

"Good morning to you too!"

"You have your appointment today, right?"

"Heading there now," Tonya said. "Where are you?"

"At work."

"Shouldn't you be doing some work then?"

"What? You're my supervisor now? Just call me when you find out something."

"Sure thing."

Keith glanced at Tonya. "She's more anxious than both of us put together."

"That's Carmen!"

—m—

Waiting to be called in for the ultrasound was nothing short of torture for Tonya. Her anxiety settled in her bladder, giving her the urge to pee.

"I hope I don't wet my pants before I'm called in," she whispered to Keith. He took her hand, gave it a quick squeeze, and reassured her that it wouldn't be too long. Tonya glanced at the clock that hung over the reception window. It was if time suddenly had stood still. Only five minutes had passed since she'd last looked at the clock, but it seemed like thirty.

The nurse finally popped her head in to call the couple in for their ultrasound. By this time Tonya was long past ready. Ignoring the room temperature, and her severe urge to use the bathroom, she braced herself for the unexpected. She'd heard all kinds of stories about mishaps during the ultrasound, such as the machine going on the blink not being able to see the sex of the baby because it wasn't in a favorable position, or expectant mothers not drinking enough water for the technician to see the image clearly. The thought of any of these things happening sent Tonya's anxiety up three notches. As the technician applied the cold gel to her belly, she whispered a prayer for a crystal clear image of the baby.

Holding her breath, Tonya couldn't believe what she saw. Her baby was moving and kicking. Tears flowed as she realized that growing inside her was a little person, not a blob or some unformed creature, as her imagination had led her believe. The technician explained to the couple each part of the baby as he pulled up the images. Tonya saw the baby's tiny ribs, ears, fingers, and toes, and the silhouette of its face. The baby's head look disproportionally larger than its tiny twelve week old body. *You've got six more months to grow into your head kid.* Tonya thought as she watched the hyperactive fetus bounce around.

The technician pointed to the location of the heart and lungs. Finally he announced to the

anxious couple, "It's a boy!"

Keith gave Tonya a hug. "It's a boy!"

He was so excited that he didn't realize Tonya was quiet. She had hoped for a girl and had wanted to name the baby after her mother. You couldn't name a boy Bethany, unless you wanted him to get his butt kicked on the playground every day of his life. Even so, Tonya took joy in knowing that the baby was a gift from God. *Lord, just let him be healthy*, Tonya prayed.

Later that day, when Tonya went over to Carmen's house and told her the news, Carmen rambled on and on about what she wanted to buy the baby, since she now knew it was a boy. "I'm going to throw your baby shower, and I'll make sure you get only the items you need. Daddy is going to be so excited. Let's call him!"

"Carmen, don't you think you should let me do something?"

"I'm letting you have the baby! What more do you want?" Carmen teased.

"You're such a clown!" Tonya said, squeezing her sister's arm.

The two women already were inseparable; this pregnancy would bring them even closer.

When they called their father to tell him the news, Tonya could hardly contain herself, and neither could her father.

"The joy of a child is God's way of telling us he's pleased with our presence. There could be no other reason that God would want to duplicate us if he didn't enjoy the relationship we have with him." Elder Lacey was so excited about the news that he suggested the three of them grab a quick lunch. Since Keith had gone back to work, and Carmen had taken the afternoon off to celebrate with Tonya, it left the two women time to spend the day with their father.

"Your treat!" Carmen announced.

"Would you have it any other way?" Elder Lacey asked with a chuckle.

14

"Congrats, man!" Brian said, raising his glass of orange juice. Keith had been so excited that he couldn't wait to tell his friends the news. He immediately had called Brian and Jerry and asked them to meet him after work to celebrate. The men met at IHOP, since it was late when Jerry finally off work.

"Now what, Pops?" Jerry asked Keith, as he placed his coffee cup on the table. "Have you two picked out a name besides 'Junior'?"

Keith looked at his friend and shook his head. The man could down a whole pot of coffee and go straight to sleep afterward.

"We haven't gotten that far yet, but what's wrong with my name?"

"Every male in your family has it!" Jerry blurted.

"Yeah," Brian said. "Who wants to be called 'Junior Junior'?"

"You're so funny! He'd be the third," Keith said

"Who wants to be called 'Third'?" Jerry said with a chuckle.

Keith sat back in his seat. "That would be messed up, but wouldn't he be called 'Trey'?"

"Give it a rest, man! You can name your kid whatever you like," Jerry said. "I'm just giving you a hard time."

"I'm happy for you. It's not every day that a man becomes a father, especially not in this group," Brian said

"Yeah, you guys need to find women and settle down too."

"Never!" Jerry said with a laugh.

"I'll settle down when I'm seventy-five and too old to party!" Brian joked.

The truth was, Brian wasn't one to party much; he just hadn't met Ms. Right. He'd had no real luck in the dating department and was just happy to hang tight with Ms. Right Now.

Keith had been trying to get his friends to join the marriage gang since his wedding day, but it had been a bust. Those guys didn't know what settling down meant, and they had no intentions of finding out.

Jerry noticed Keith looking toward the front door of the restaurant after briefly checking his vibrating phone. Looking annoyed, Jerry asked, "You got plans?"

"No, I just gotta get back home. Unlike you two, I'm a married man."

"Well, that's odd coming from you, young stud," Brian quipped.

"Hey, I gotta run, but I'll meet up with you guys later," Keith said, after checking his cell phone.

Once he got to his car, he frowned at the number before slipping the phone back into its holster. Shayla had been blowing up his phone all evening. Even after he had yelled at her to stop calling him, she continued. He hated having this type of distraction when Tonya was pregnant. Turning his cell phone off, Keith sped home.

⎯⎯ℳ⎯⎯

Sister Peggy's voice was three octaves above her usual high-pitched voice as she excitedly expressed her exuberance over the news of the baby's sex. Tonya had to call her, since she was like a second mother to her. Sister Peggy had been in Tonya's life for as long as she could remember. After Tonya's mother had died, Sister Peggy had been right there to comfort her. She had taken it upon herself to look after the Lacey family.

"Oh, Tonya, I can imagine a little Elder Lacey running around the church!"

"I'm sure Daddy could use someone to keep him busy, especially since he's never had a son of his own."

"God knows what we need, doesn't he, child?"

"Ain't that the truth? Even when we don't think it's what we want, God knows our needs."

Sister Peggy was as excited as Carmen, promising to help Tonya pick out the baby's bed over the weekend. Tonya couldn't bring herself to tell Sister

Peggy that Carmen had taken over that duty as well. Carmen had done just about everything the mother-to-be was supposed to do. Carmen had told her in no uncertain terms that her duty was simply to have the baby.

"Carmen's planning a baby shower in a couple of months, so be prepared to make your famous seven-cheese pound cake," Tonya said.

"I'll do better than that. I'll cater for ya!"

"Thanks, Sister Peggy, but Carmen has that covered already."

"Well, I guess Carmen's got this all figured out. Ain't much left for me to do, is there?" she asked, sounded dejected.

"You certainly can cook for me once I have the baby. Your cooking is off the chain!"

"I can bake you a nice casserole, and I already know you love my pound cake!"

Tonya laughed at the older woman's enthusiasm. "You're getting started a little early, huh?""Well, you know what they say, 'If you fail to plan, you plan to fail,' and I can't have my cake failing all over the place."

Tonya knew Sister Peggy meant well, but her rationale just flew out the window. Shaking her head, she let Sister Peggy ramble about the meals she was planning to prepare for her after the baby came home. Everyone was making such a fuss over her, but it did make her feel special. Tonya felt Sister Peggy was a member of the family as much as her dad and Carmen were. She couldn't imagine her life any other way.

15

"Come on, man. Play your hand already!" Brian yelled across the table at Keith.

Keith moaned. "Sorry, my mind is somewhere else." Checking out the cards before him, he couldn't tell who had played what card, so he threw down a king to match the queen that lay on the table.

Reaching to collect the card, Jerry rolled his eyes. "Pay attention, man. You just wasted a book. That was my queen, fool!"

"My bad."

"Either you play or walk. A betting man would kill you over something like that."

"Do the words 'My bad' mean anything anymore?"

"Yeah, but not today. Now play!"

Keith shook his head and threw down the five of diamonds.

As the cards made their way around the table, Jay excitedly plopped down the king of diamonds, causing the card to spin on the table. "I'll take that! Don't play wit me, boy! I am da man!" He settled down, slid the ten of hearts on the table, and waited for his card to get snatched away. The cards made their way around the table again. Having nothing higher in his hand, Keith threw down a seven of hearts.

All the while Jay was yelling, "Stand up! Ten! Stand up! Ten!"

The guys had met at Jay's apartment, since it was his night to host their card game. Jay was Brian's cousin and ,worked as a fireman. He had played college football but was injured during his sophomore year. His grades weren't the best either, so he'd left college, licked his wounds, and became a firefighter. He was an overall fun guy, but modesty wasn't one of his strong suits. The dude would brag about throwing a piece of paper in the wastebasket if he thought it would get him recognition.

Feeling his cell phone vibrate at his side, Keith tilted his hip in his chair as he leaned over to get a view of the caller ID. *Dang, what does she want now?* he asked himself. He decided not to answer the call in front of the guys and let the call roll over to his voice mail. He didn't want to endure the brutality the guys would subject him to if they knew Shayla was calling him.

As Keith fidgeted in his chair, Brian picked up on the change in his demeanor. "Why won't you answer the phone, K.J.?"

"Oh, it's nobody. I'll just let it go to voice mail." Attempting to redirect the guys' attention to the game, he asked, "Whose play is it, anyway?"

Keith was having a hard time trying to keep Shayla from calling him. It had been three weeks since he had walked away from their relationship, and she constantly called him. What did he have to do to get this girl to leave him alone? Not wanting to deal with Shayla's constant pestering and stalking, Keith had stopped taking her calls. This only made her angry, which had led to a barrage of nasty, insulting, and threatening messages on his voice mail. Just last week she had left three voice mails with the same message, "Your day will come. Just wait!" Keith didn't know what to make of these odd and coded messages. Was she planning on doing something crazy, like stop by his job, drive by his house, or hell, maybe even do a drive-by shooting? He didn't know what to expect with this girl. He never should have told her where he worked. Was she going to call his wife and reveal their little escapade? Keith couldn't keep his mind on the game.

Brian sat quietly, watching Keith fight with his emotions. Not wanting to draw any attention to his friend's demeanor, he knew he'd have to wait to talk to him alone. Feeling the heat from his spades partner, Keith decided to end his torment and call it a night.

"Next time come to play or stay at home!" Jay said.

"Exactly!" Jerry added. "Come to play or stay at home."

Keith grabbed his jacket from the back of his chair. "Got it, man," he told Jerry. "I'm just glad you left your gat at home."

The men laughed at the thought of Jerry ready to shoot to kill.

"Call a brutha later, man," Brian yelled, then headed to the back of the house to the bathroom.

"Sure thing," Keith said, as he walked out the door.

Later that evening Keith called Brian. He needed to relieve some of the burden he was carrying. For the past few weeks, he'd been trying to deal with the fact that he had created a fatal attraction in his marriage. He didn't know how to get rid of Shayla without Tonya finding out about her.

After Keith poured out his heart to his friend, he felt a great deal of relief.

"Man, I really messed up!" Keith whispered into the receiver. He had waited until Tonya was asleep before he had called Brian.

"My mom used to tell me, 'You've made your bed. Now you've got to lie in it.' So since you've made your bed, fix it. Don't let your mistake ruin your marriage."

"That's what I thought I was doing when I kicked Shayla's butt to the curb, but she won't let me go."

Brian sighed. "I know I sound like a broken record, but again I say, 'Fix it!' Make her let you go. Don't lose a good woman like Tonya over someone like that."

Keith held the phone away from his ear, listening for Tonya.

"Hello?" Brian spoke into the phone.

"Sorry. I'm here. I thought I heard Tonya get up. Look, I've got to go. I'd hate for her to wake up and catch me whispering on the phone. She'd definitely think it's a woman on the other end. I'll catch you later. Thanks, B!"

"No doubt!"

16

"Carmen, you can't possibly be serious. Who'd ever think of buying a newborn a room full of toys? It'll be a while before he can even play with half of this stuff."

Tonya laughed as Carmen came in bearing an armful of stuffed animals, gadgets, and trinkets. She was known to overdo everything she did, and shopping was one of those things.

"There's more in the trunk of my car," she said, as she placed the toys on the couch.

"While you were out shopping, did you think about the mother-to-be?"

"Why, of course!" Carmen said, pulling out a small pearl-colored box with a ribbon tied around it and presenting it to her sister.

Tonya became as giddy as a teenage girl as she opened the gift.

"It's beautiful! Thanks, Carmen." She held up the gold bracelet that had been engraved. It read, "To Tonya, my sis and BFF. Love, C.L."

Tonya hugged her sister tightly and smiled. At this moment she realized she'd never felt more loved.

"Well, we'd better hurry. Daddy can't stand for us to be late," Carmen said, as she grabbed her purse. The women had to meet with Elder Lacey for their weekly lunch.

This was a tradition Elder Lacey had begun once his daughters had started college. Each week the trio met to discuss events in their lives, both good and bad.

As Elder Lacey sat across the table from his girls, his eyes sparkled as he beamed with pride. "I only wish your mother could be here to share in the joy of your having a child, Tonya."

Tears formed at the corners of his eyes. Fighting them back, he dabbed at his eyes with a napkin and gave Tonya a smile. Elder Lacey never had made his girls feel any less loved despite his deep wish for a son. He and Bethany had planned to have a boy and a girl, but when he was blessed with two daughters, he was pleased with what God had given him. Over the years his daughters had brought him so much joy, and he was grateful for having them in his life.

His voice cracked with emotion. "Your mother would be so proud."

"I know that Mom is smiling down on us now and that she's proud of all of us." Tonya felt her mother's presence as she sat eating lunch with her beloved father and sister.

17

Tonya had just revealed to Keith the diagnosis the doctor had given her a week earlier. She didn't tell him immediately because she simply didn't know how to break such devastating news. She had hoped she would receive a call back saying the test results were a mistake. All the while she had prayed, "Lord, grant me a miracle," but she received no such call.

"How the hell did you think I'd react when you bring me some crap like this? What did you do, Tonya, sleep with half the men at that fake church you attend, or was it half the men at your job?" Keith yelled as he crossed the room. He grabbed a vase and tossed it in her direction, missing her by mere inches.

This wasn't the reaction Tonya had expected. She had received the same news a week earlier, yet she didn't get as angry as Keith was right now.

Keith had completely destroyed the living room, throwing pictures and other objects. He picked up a lamp near the couch and hurled it across the room, shattering Tonya's prized full-length mirror. She watched as shards of glass littered the floor. She stood crying in the corner, trembling with fear, hoping Keith would leave and not take his anger out on her next.

He went on a rampage for two hours, tearing apart the house, breaking anything that wasn't tied down. Terrified, Tonya sprinted toward the front door. Keith saw her quick movement and rushed to prevent her from leaving.

"Where do you think you're going?" he asked, as he snatched her by her hair and dragged her back into the living room.

Struggling to free herself from his grip only enraged Keith more. Each time Tonya struggled, he tightened his grip. Keith dragged Tonya from one room to the other; all the while she suffered cuts and scrapes from the broken glass on the floor. Begging Keith to let her go sent him to a new level of rage, as he slammed his fist into Tonya's left eye. Her vision became blurry, and the pain jolted her into a realization that there was more to come. Tonya took a quick survey of the room in an attempt to locate her car keys. She spotted them on the hook near the door and waited for the chance to get away from her crazed husband. A visual flashed before her of women in horror movies falling while being chased by a serial killer; she could see Keith standing over her, brutally taking her life from her. Tonya tried to muster the strength to break free, but it was fruitless. The more Keith pounded his fist into her flesh, the less she felt the blows. She felt a sense of doom as she began to lose consciousness. She could no longer hear Keith's slurs and insults as he battered her. It was if her spirit had left her body.

Keith lost his grip as she slid to the floor.

As Tonya began to regain her senses, she hear Keith's heavy breathing near her as he paced back and forth, cursing her existence. She quietly listened as his footsteps grew distant. Fear kept her from opening her eyes, but she could tell he was no longer standing over her. Peering through the slits of her eyes, she saw Keith's image near the kitchen. Her heart began to quicken, and she feared he could hear her raging pulse as it echoed in her ears. The thought of the multitude of weapons he could use crossed her mind. After gathering her last bit of strength, Tonya jumped up, raced across the room, grabbed her keys, and sprinted out the door. She heard Keith yelling behind her. *Oh, God,* she thought. *He's crazy. He's trying to kill me.* She fumbled with the car key as she raced to the vehicle. Activating the lock, she jumped behind the wheel, slipped the key into the ignition, and quickly put the car into reverse.

"Where are you going? You get back here! I'm not through with you!" Keith yelled from the doorway as Tonya sped away.

Tonya was frantic as she drove down the highway. She kept looking back to see if Keith had followed her; he was mad enough to kill her. After checking her speedometer, which read ninety-seven, she eased her foot off the gas and allowed the car to slow down to seventy. She checked her rearview mirror again—no Keith. Her heart was racing, and her adrenalin had kicked into overdrive and had taken over her senses. She was driving on autopilot. Her sense of direction had abandoned her; she had missed her exit and had to get off on the next one so she could turn around. She had no idea where she was going; she had left her cell phone and purse at home, so had to make due with the gas she had.

Her mouth stung as the salty tears slid down her battered face. She touched the corner of her mouth and quickly jerked her hand from her injured lip. Even without looking in the mirror, she knew her face was swollen.

—⁂—

Keith's rage elevated to another level after Tonya had escaped. *The nerve of her trying to leave me after she tells me she's got HIV and that I need to be tested.* He paced the floor, imagining the multitude of trysts Tonya had probably had over the past eight years of their marriage.

That's probably not even my baby! he thought. *What else has she been up to? All those nights she claimed to be at choir rehearsal, going to prayer meetings, going to the hospital to visit sick church members, and trying to help the pastor rebuild the youth facility.* Keith snatched the wedding album from the coffee table and tore the pictures into pieces as he thought of his wife sleeping with another man.

"Liar! You lying wench!" he yelled, as he picked up one of their framed wedding pictures that showed a beautiful smiling bride walking down the aisle. He threw the photo to the floor and stomped on it, crushing the glass beneath his foot.

Focusing on a picture of their first kiss as husband and wife, he stared at Tonya's face intensely. "Tramp!" he yelled, ripping the picture to shreds.

"I should have left you years ago!" he screamed, as he tossed the wedding album into the fireplace, intending to erase their entire marriage.

He lit a match, tossed it into the fireplace, and watched Tonya's smiling face become distorted as it burned. He wanted nothing more than to forget the one day he regretted the most, the day he'd said, "I do."

Knowing Tonya probably had gone to Carmen's house, he contemplated driving over there to finish what he had started. Instead he picked up the phone and called Jerry. He needed to talk to his boys before he did something crazy enough to land him in prison. When Jerry answered, Keith's mouth went completely dry. As if his mouth held cotton balls, he couldn't speak.

"Hello?" Jerry said in to the phone but got no answer. Jerry had seen Keith's name flash across the phone, but he couldn't hear him. "Hello?" Jerry repeated. "Are you there?"

After three "hellos" from Jerry, Keith finally let out a whimper. "Jerry, hey, man. It's Keith. We need to talk." Keith couldn't take "no" for an answer and was glad when Jerry said now was a good time. Keith decided to drive over to Jerry's house, because he had practically destroyed his own home.

After talking to Jerry, Keith called Brian, who had just gotten back in town from visiting his grandmother, who was recently hospitalized.

"Hey, man. What's going on?" Brian spoke cheerfully into the phone.

"I'll tell you about it when I see you. Just come over to Jerry's, and don't take all day. I got some serious madness to get off my chest!"

18

Keith reluctantly revealed to his friends the news that Tonya had laid on him. He waited for a reaction from them, hoping they'd understand his anguish. The two men sat quietly for several moments before either spoke.

Jerry leaned forward in his chair and opened his mouth, but the only thing he could muster was a groan. The silence was killing Keith. Usually the guys would jump on a chance to give their advice or show support, but they said nothing.

Brian finally spoke. "Have you gone to the doctor yet?"

"Naw, man. I just found out before I called you guys."

"You need to go see a doctor as soon as possible. It's not like she told you she has the measles or something."

Jerry flipped a quarter through his fingers. "HIV? You know, Crackhead Joe had that mess. Before he died, he was skin and bones, and his eyes were sunken in like they didn't belong in his head, and he—"

"Yeah, but I'm not a crackhead, man! I don't do drugs, and definitely not crack! So don't compare me to Crackhead Joe!"

Brian didn't like the fact that Keith had accused his wife of infidelity. He wondered whether what his friend was telling him was indeed true. He had known Keith for a long time, and he knew it didn't take much to excite his friend when it came to women. All it took was a little flirting, and Keith would forget all about the wife he had at home.

"How do you know she gave it to you?" Brian asked. "Tonya is so devoted to that church she goes to. I can't see her cheating on you."

Keith stood up. "What's that supposed to mean? Man, who goes to church five days a week? There ain't that much church in the world!"

"All I'm saying is that she's a church girl. You knew that when you married her. Her dad's a preacher, and they were raised in the church. She just doesn't fit the profile of that kind of woman."

"Well, she's not doing much at home. Somebody's getting her attention, and it sure as hell ain't me! I can count on one hand how many times we make love in a month, and it's poorly done to say the least!" Keith barked.

Jerry and Brian exchanged glances, each thinking about the fact that Keith was the one who had stepped out on Tonya. They knew how flirtatious Keith could be whenever the three of them went out for drinks. You'd think he was the single one in the group.

"Man, I was so mad when she told me that I wanted to kill her! I tore the house up and beat the hell out of that trifling ho before she got away!"

"You hit your wife?" Jerry shouted in disbelief; his eyes doubled in size.

"I just lost it!"

"Is she OK? You know she's pregnant," Brian said.

"She's OK. I didn't do what I really wanted to do, so she'll live."

"You'd just better hope she's OK and hope she doesn't press charges." Jerry stood and walked over to the window. "There's no excuse for putting your hands on a woman, especially a pregnant woman."

"I don't know what came over me. I was so angry."

"As your boy, I feel I can say this," Brian said. "That's a lame excuse. You were wrong."

"I said I didn't mean to do it." Keith stood up.

Brian shook his head. "Look, I've been your boy for a long time, and I've known your wife just as long, so I just can't believe you would blame Tonya for anything like this. She's not the type of person to step out like that. You need to check your facts, kid, because if I'm not mistaken, you're the one doing wrong!"

"Man, forget this! I have feelings too. What about me? She comes home and lays this on me and expects me to understand? You two sound like Dumb and Dumber sitting here telling me how to react!" Grabbing his car keys off the coffee table, Keith headed toward the door. "If I find her, I'm gonna kill her!"

—⚏—

Driving down the highway at breakneck speed, Keith was both suicidal and homicidal as he relived the last minutes he'd spent with his friends. He was upset that Brian and Jerry didn't see things his way, and hurt that they were more concerned about Tonya than they were about him.

How dare they judge me after what I've just endured? he thought. *What kind of friends are they to instantly take Tonya's side over mine? With friends like those two, who needs enemies?*

Keith mimicked Brian's last statement. "As your boy, I feel I can say this. That's a lame excuse. You were wrong."

He tried to rationalize his actions over the last few hours and wondered how his friends could take Tonya's side. She had just come home and told him she'd given him a death sentence, and they expected him to be OK with that. Tonya probably knew all along that she was sick, and now she wanted to lay this in his lap, as if having a baby would make things better.

In a blind fit of rage and mixed emotions, Keith ran through a red light, barely missing an SUV as the driver swerved to avoid his vehicle. The driver laid on his horn as Keith flew past him, pausing briefly to throw a barrage of insults at Keith before continuing on his way.

Not noticing the near miss, he continued to rant about his friends' failure to have his back. "Maybe that's the problem. You're not really my boys," Keith said as he slapped the steering wheel in anger.

19

As Tonya pulled into Carmen's driveway, she felt numb and emotionally drained. How on earth could she explain this situation to her sister, who would most certainly, without hesitation, call her dad the minute she saw her battered face and tattered clothes? Touching her swollen eye, Tonya knew she couldn't hide it any longer. As she reached to open the car door, she winced in pain. Her ribs felt as if they were on fire, and the blood vessels in her head throbbed so hard that she felt as if her head might explode.

Willing herself to get out of the car, she slid off the seat, ignoring the pain that seized her with the slightest movement. Each breath sent pain searing through her chest, and each step took sheer determination. She wrapped her arms around her waist to constrict the expansion of her diaphragm. This seemed to alleviate the pain as she gingerly made her way up the driveway. Preparing for the worst, Tonya took slow, deliberate breaths. With each shallow breath she inhaled a small amount of air, holding it with each step. She exhaled slowly as she pressed the doorbell.

Hearing the musical chimes of the doorbell, Carmen quickly turned down the fire on the stove. After running to the door and looking out the window, she saw Tonya's car parked out front. She quickly unlocked the door and rushed back to the stove as she yelled, "Come on in!"

Tonya carefully entered the house, every muscle in her body aching.

"Hey, big sis! How's the mother-to-be?" Carmen called from the kitchen as Tonya entered the house. "Girl, come on into the kitchen. I'm cooking dinner. What's brings you this way? You usually call before coming over. Just be glad I'm a homebody."

Tonya didn't know how to start this conversation. *How do you tell someone you love that you're dying?* she wondered. Tears welled in her eyes; unable to control herself any longer, she cried openly.

Carmen stopped stirring her pot and turned to Tonya with raised eyebrows. "What's going on? Is it the baby?" When she walked over to her sister and saw her face for the first time, a shriek escaped her lips as her heart sank. "Tonya, what happened to you? Look at your face! Did Keith do this to you?"

"We had a fight, and things got out of hand. He didn't mean to—he was upset. I had to tell him…"

"Tonya, stop making excuses for him! How many times has he done this?"

"Never. It was just this one time."

"Are you hurt? Is the baby hurt?"

Tonya shook her head. "I look worse than I feel."

"You've got to tell Daddy. Did you call the police? Why did he put his hands on you, a pregnant woman? What gives him the right?" Carmen grabbed the cordless phone from its charger and began to dial.

"No, please don't bring Daddy or the police into this. I don't want this to get out of hand."

"It's past out of hand, and it's not like Dad's not going to notice that cartoon-looking eye you're sporting."

In a panic Tonya ran to the mirror to assess the damage to her face. "Oh, no!" she shrieked. She couldn't believe what she saw. Her left eye was a mess; it was almost completely shut and had a dark purple hue that couldn't be mistaken for anything else but a black eye. "I can't leave the house like this!" she exclaimed.

As Carmen filled a plastic freezer bag with ice and handed it to Tonya, she noticed her hands were trembling; she was livid. "I've got a mind to go over there and whip him like the punk he is!" Carmen said as she sat down. "Stay here for as long as you like. You can't go back there. He could end up killing you and the baby."

Overwhelmed with emotions, Tonya tried to explain herself between sobs. "I'm sick, Carmen, I'm…" Unable to finish her sentence, she collapsed into a chair at the kitchen table.

Carmen cradled her sister in her arms. "Tonya, what's wrong? Have you been to the doctor? Have you been taking your prenatal vitamins? Those vitamins will help you have a healthy baby. Maybe you should—"

Cutting Carmen off, Tonya blurted out, "Carmen, I have HIV! Prenatal vitamins won't cure this. Hell, antibiotics won't cure this!"

Carmen's mouth flew open; Tonya's announcement had left her speechless. After a few moments, she could only muster a feeble, "Are you sure?"

Tonya nodded.

"How could this be? You don't do drugs. You're married and a faithful Christian. How could this happen?"

Tonya began to shed fresh tears. The look on Carmen's face drained her of any courage she had left. News of this magnitude would destroy her dad.

"What the damn hell am I supposed to do?" Tonya clamped a hand over her mouth as the expletives flew from her lips. "Lord, forgive me for swearing like a drunken sailor. I don't know what came over me."

"Tonya, I'm sure God will forgive you for that, because technically that wasn't swearing." Carmen laughed softly at her sister's attempt at using profanity.

"Who made you the queen of profanity, Miss Thang? Don't let Daddy know you've been cursing!"

"Anyone who uses 'damn' and 'hell' together shouldn't try using profanity. I'm sure God is laughing at you too."

Tonya dismissed her sister's joke with a wave of her hand. "Keith stepped outside of our marriage—I'm sure of it. He violated my temple with a disease that's incurable, but he blames me. I'd rather be told I have gonorrhea or herpes...but HIV? He'd have done better by shooting me dead in the street, because he just took my life! Being a Christian isn't enough, not when you're sleeping with the enemy."

Carmen felt numb. How could her sister be the victim of such a deadly disease?

"I didn't think married people got HIV," Tonya said with a sigh.

"Tonya, no one is immune from HIV, not even married people." Carmen slammed her fist onto the table. "This really pisses me off! How could a man who claims to love you do something so awful as to cheat on you and not even have enough sense to use a condom to protect you? If that's love, I can just imagine what hate looks like." Carmen looked into Tonya's puffy, red, tear-streaked face. "What about the baby?"

Tonya had thought about that often over the past week. H How could she bring a child into the world only to potentially give it a death sentence?

"I talked to Dr. Gipson," she said. "He mentioned something about my taking AZT to help prevent the baby from getting the virus."

Carmen appeared alarmed. "Is that medicine safe for the baby? Most doctors warn against pregnant women taking anything but Tylenol, and AZT is a lot stronger than Tylenol."

" He gave me some literature on the drug. He said it's safest to take after the first trimester, and it's helped save babies from contracting the virus, but I'm no expert and who really knows for sure."

"Tonya, I know we've been raised in the church and don't believe in abortions, but do you really want to have this baby, knowing it might get HIV and die?"

Carmen wasn't suggesting anything Tonya hadn't already thought about at least a thousand times since learning of her diagnosis. "I've thought about that, but right now I'm just trying to get through each day—you know, taking it one day at a time."

The two sisters sat together for a while, holding each other while crying and praying that they'd wake up from this nightmare.

Taking a sip of the steaming hot coffee before her, Tonya fumed over the fight she'd had with Keith. In all the years of their marriage, he'd never raised a hand to her. Touching her face sent shockwaves through her already aching body. It probably would take a couple of weeks before the bruises and swelling subsided. She'd have to come up with some pretty convincing tales to cover up her absence from work, church, and choir rehearsal. Unfortunately no excuse she could come up with, no matter how ingenious, would keep her father from seeing her battered face. Elder Lacy made it a routine to spend at least two days a week with his daughters, lunch during the week and church on Sunday, and he didn't take "no" for an answer.

Tonya and Carmen ate dinner with minimum conversation. Unanswered questions lingered in the air, and Tonya needed resolution. After dinner she decided to take a walk in the park to sort out the situation that had been thrown into her lap.

"Want some company?" Carmen asked.

"No, I need a few minutes alone. I need to talk to God. I've got questions only He can answer."

After borrowing a navy blue cardigan from her sister, Tonya stepped into the cool night air to clear her head. As she thought about her situation, she became increasing angry with herself for marrying Keith, angry with Keith for giving her HIV and blaming her, and angry with God.

"What kind of God would allow this to happen to me?" Tonya screamed. "I serve you, Lord. Why are you allowing this to happen to me?" She heard only the stillness of the park and felt the heat from the rage she held within. *How could he be in denial about how I got the virus?* she thought. *I'd never do anything to put either of us in harm.*

Taking a seat on a park bench, she put her head in her hands and cried. As she sat in sorrow, she suddenly felt a small, still presence. Looking up she saw no one, but she knew someone was with her. Feeling a sense of calm and peace in the still of the night, she felt God's presence.

Tonya wiped her tears. She knew God had not forsaken her.

20

Unable to sleep her problems away, Tonya opened her eyes as the sun beamed down on her puffy face. She gently touched her face and moaned at the thought of what she must look like this morning. The tissue around her swollen eye was soft and filled with fluid. Her bottom lip had doubled in size, and the corner of her lips was hard, as the cut attempted to seal and form a scab. She knew without looking in the mirror that her face looked like a horror show. With nowhere to go and no energy to get up, she decided to stay in bed. As she rolled over, she felt a wet sticky substance on her inner thighs and underwear that had , soaked through her thin nightgown. Jerking the covers back, she noticed a pink stain on her clothes.

"Oh, my God. My baby!" Tonya screamed. "God, please save my baby!" She jumped out of bed and sprinted to Carmen's bedroom. "Carmen, wake up. I need to go to the hospital!"

On the drive to the hospital, Tonya prayed she'd make it in time to save her baby. At that moment she knew she couldn't abort her baby; she felt love for the child growing inside her. It seemed as if everything was going wrong.

Is God punishing me for something I did? she wondered. *Did I place a curse on my baby's life by being angry with God?* Tonya wanted to take back every accusatory remark she'd made to God while blaming Him for her predicament. She repented and asked God to save her unborn child. Panic seared her as they traveled to the hospital.

Looking at the speedometer, Carmen saw she was going seventy miles an hour, but it seemed as if she were crawling at thirty.

When they arrived at the hospital and the staff questioned Tonya about the bruises on her body and face, she felt conflicted. She couldn't tell them the truth—Keith could end up in jail yet she blamed him for putting her baby's life in jeopardy.

"I fell." The lie felt bitter as it rolled off her tongue. She immediately felt mixed emotions about lying.

"How many times did you fall, Mrs. Paris?" one of the nurses asked. "Because your injuries are inconsistent with your story. Would you like to be truthful, or would you like for me to contact the police?"

"No! Look, the truth is…I had a fight with my husband. I left home shortly afterward. I'll be fine. Please don't get anyone involved."

"I really need to report this, Mrs. Paris."

"I'd appreciate it if you didn't. I'm no longer in danger."

The nurse bit her bottom lip as if considering Tonya's request. She scribbled something on Tonya's chart, gave her a slight nod, then left the room.

Feeling overwhelmed with guilt about the lie she'd told, Tonya mumbled a word of repentance under her breath. She'd hate for the police to be called, which probably would result in Keith being hauled off to jail. She nervously nibbled at a hangnail on her index finger.

Carmen sits on the edge of the small hospital bed. "You should have knocked the hell out of him."

Tonya rolled her eyes. "And what good would that have done? It would have only made matters worse."

"I might have lost the fight, but it wouldn't be due to a lack of trying."

"Carmen, women can't go around trying to manhandle men."

"You're on that turn the other check bull and I aint that saved. We must have skipped that chapter in Sunday School because the only cheek I'd be turning is Keith's as I beat the hell out of him."

"Violence begets violence."

"That's why it's called a fight."

"You're hopeless."

"Do you remember when Bobby Sloan tried to bully me in the fourth grade?"

"Yes I do."

"Well, after I tried to break him in half he never bothered me again."

"Carmen, you broke the boy's nose!"

"Well, that fixed him didn't it?"

"And if I recall correctly, daddy tried to fix you as well." Tonya laughed as she reflected on how their father chased Carmen around the house with a belt.

Tonya endured six hours of observation and drank what felt like a gallon of water and juice, only to be told that tests confirmed she was leaking amniotic fluid. She was instructed to go home and rest.

Rest? she thought. *How can I rest when my life has been turned upside down?*

"What about the leak?" Tonya asked the nurse.

"It should seal on its own. Keep drinking plenty of fluids, and take it easy."

She tried to look on the bright side; at least her baby was doing fine. The nurse said the baby's heartbeat was steady at 160 beats a minute. After she reassured her that this was a normal heartbeat for a fetus, Tonya felt she could sleep easier.

As she signed her discharge papers, Tonya felt relieved that no one had called the police. She did, however, have to speak to a social worker. The woman was very understanding and was satisfied that Tonya had left the home and had a support system with Carmen.

Once she got back to Carmen's house, Tonya was dead tired, but she knew she had to call Sister Peggy. She knew Sister Peggy would try to call her at home or on her cell phone, and Keith probably wouldn't be too nice to her if he answered the phone.

"I've been thinking about you and hoping everything is going well. I've tried to reach you at home but kept getting your answering machine. How's the baby coming along?" Sister Peggy asked in her usual upbeat voice.

Tonya didn't have the heart to break the news to Sister Peggy just yet. "We're fine. I'm spending a few days with my sister. The doctor put me on bed rest since I had a little setback, but it's nothing to worry about."

"You sound so downtrodden. What's wrong?"

"I'm just tired." Tonya knew Sister Peggy wasn't buying her story; she knew Tonya too well.

"Well, dear heart, call me when you feel up to talking. I'll keep you in my prayers."

"Thanks. I'll call you later in the week."

"OK, just remember that God won't put more on us than we can bear." Sister Peggy always quoted little adages she thought would get a person through anything. Her favorite was, "It's only a test, so don't give up and flunk out on God!"

Tonya never had understood where Sister Peggy got her quotes, because she'd never read them anywhere in the Bible, but they'd served her well over the years.

Knowing Keith would be at work for most of the day, Tonya and Carmen entered the house to gather as much of Tonya's belonging as they could fit in Carmen's car. Even though Keith wasn't home, Tonya felt nervous entering her home. She felt antsy and constantly looked around, as if Keith would suddenly appear around a corner. Tonya's home no longer felt like her home, and walking back into the space sent a cold chill down her spine. The broken glass was no longer on the floor, but she noticed that all their pictures had been taken down from the walls, mantle, and end tables. It was if Keith wanted to erase her from his life. Tonya headed for her bedroom to retrieve her clothes; she hoped he hadn't tossed her things in the trash.1

She held up a beige suit with a blue-and-an scarf around the collar and briefly, thought about taking it with her.

"I don't remember seeing you in that one. How nice!" Carmen said, as she stroked the beautifully designed buttons that adorned the front of the suit.

"And you won't! It was a gift from Keith after one of our recent fights."

"How much of a fight was it? Was it a yelling match or an Ike and Tina fight?"

"Let's not get into that right now. It's not important."

Taking her sister's hands in hers, Carmen pulled Tonya around to face her "It is important," she said, "especially if you've been hiding bruises and black eyes."

"The bruises I wear aren't visible."

The two women sat on the edge of the bed as Tonya spilled the details of Keith's late nights, which he claimed he'd spent hanging out with Jerry or Brian. One night, when Keith was out late, Tonya had called Keith's cell phone; Keith told her not to wait up for him because he was at Jerry's, watching the fight. She took it upon herself to drive by Jerry's house to see for herself. When she stopped in front of the house, she saw that Jerry was home, since his bedroom light was on, and the light from the TV was flickering. Keith's car, however, was nowhere in sight. Tonya dialed Jerry's number, maybe Keith had forgotten to warn him that he had used him as an alibi. Jerry said Keith wasn't with him and told her to try Brian. No need to try Brian; she had seen him earlier that evening, leaving his house with a young woman on his arm—"going out to paint the town red," as he'd said. Fuming from her discovery, Tonya drove home in tears.

"Why didn't you leave him then?" Carmen asked. "Maybe you wouldn't have gotten sick."

"Because I prayed about the situation and left it in God's hands."

"Tonya! God gave us free will. He won't make you stay if the other person doesn't love you the way you deserve to be loved."

"I made a vow. You wouldn't understand. You've never been married. It's not as simple as ending a dating relationship."

"I understand that, but you weren't the only one who made a vow. If this is what a vow means, I'll gladly live without making one!"

"When you get married, you'll do whatever you can to keep your family together."

"Tonya, it takes two. You can't have a marriage by yourself. You can't keep making it so easy for him. Kick him out of your life!"

"It's not that easy. When you've given someone your life, heart, and energy for so long, it becomes very hard to simply walk away. Now I don't have a choice."

"Don't talk like that. You always have a choice. Like the saying goes, better late than never. Let's just get your things and leave him to his own destruction."

With no intention of staying in an abusive marriage, Tonya hurriedly collected her belongings, leaving behind any memories of her and Keith's union. She saw the remains of her wedding album in the fireplace. *The feelings are mutual, because as far as I'm concerned, this marriage is over*, Tonya thought, as she closed the door behind her.

Carmen and Tonya's spirits improved after they left the house, and they decided to treat themselves to a day of pampering at the health spa, followed by a nice lunch. Tonya was patiently waiting for the storm to calm and the healing process to begin. She began to encourage herself, quoting her favorite scripture, Psalms 30:5, silently to herself—"Weeping may endure for a night, but joy cometh in the morning." Elder Lacey often told his girls that when things seem to be at their worst, that's when God is getting ready to bless.

Sitting across from each other during lunch, Tonya and Carmen shared memories of growing up with their dad. Tonya recalled the first time a boy had called the house to speak to her. Elder Lacey had drilled the young man until he'd changed his mind about wanting to speak to Tonya at all. Tonya wasn't too disturbed by it, because it was just Clay, a boy who sat behind her in English class. Clay had halitosis to the core. She hated when Mrs. Jarvis, her English teacher, asked him a question or asked him to read aloud. It was as if she could smell every syllable, and to make matters worse, Clay had a lisp and sprayed her when he talked. She felt as if sewer water were raining down on her.

As they reminisced, the women no longer had adult problems, they were now school-age girls with school-age problems.

"Do you remember the first sermon Pastor Dobbs preached at New Covenant?" Tonya asked Carmen, trying to hold back her laughter.

"Yeah, who could forget 'Don't let the devil steal yo' shoes?'"

The women cracked up as they remembered Pastor Dobbs and his way with words.

"He was trying to pronounce 'scriptures,' but he kept saying 'striptures' and 'obstickels' for 'obstacles.' He hemmed and hawed so much that he got dehydrated." Tears escaped Carmen's eyes as she recounted Pastor Dobbs' sermons. "I hated when he preached. No one understood half the words he said!"

The women continued to talk and laugh at the fiascos that had taken place at New Covenant over the years. Hating to kill the moment, Carmen became worried about Tonya when she noticed that her breaths were short and choppy at times.

"How are you feeling? I've noticed you taking a lot of rest breaks when we walk, and you seem out of breath now, and we're just talking."

"I have these spells, but they don't last long. Don't worry. I'm fine."

"Have you told your doctor about them? They can't be good."

"I'll mention it to him next time, but I'm sure they're nothing."

Carmen watched Tonya as she sat across from her, eating her third cup of ice. "Tonya, do you think ice is good for you? You're going to make your iron level low with all that ice you've been eating."

"I can't help it. I crave ice like other pregnant women crave pickles and ice cream."

"When you go see your doctor, let him know your iron levels might be low and that you're always cold."

"Yeah, I'm on iron supplements, but they make me constipated" She paused and laughed lightly. "Maybe that was TMI."

"Just ease up off the ice a little, OK?"

"Sure, Mom. No more ice snacks for me!" Tonya said sarcastically.

Carmen didn't see the need to upset Tonya, especially in her condition, so she dropped the subject. Besides, why ruin the day by scaring her half to death over a few ice cubes?

"Hey, let's go catch a movie tonight. I'll buy the popcorn!"

"It's a date!" Tonya said, draining the last bit of ice chips from her cup.

21

Elder Lacey had scheduled a lunch date with his daughters in hopes of getting more information about Tonya and Keith's recent marital problems. Tonya had called her father earlier in the week to alert him of her separation from her husband but avoided giving any specific details. Carmen picked the restaurant for their weekly lunch date. She had noticed a new that opened a few weeks ago and was dying to try it. Erma's Din, a soul food restaurant was the new buzz around town. The building was erected a few blocks from New Covenant and had been flooded with church goers since their grand opening. She had heard members rave about her home made peach cobbler, macaroni and cheese that was to die for and meat loaf that melt in your mouth. Tonya mouth watered at the thought of food that awaited her.

As she stepped into the restaurant, the smell of fried chicken, fish, and collard greens greeted her. Her stomach began to churn loud enough for Carmen to hear.

"I guess someone's hungry."

"The smell has me salivating."

The place was small but quaint. Tables were placed in the only open space available.. Two or three chairs were placed around each small table, which were covered with a nylon table cloth. The food was served from behind a large counter which contained a strip of plexiglass. The food was arranged for left to right with the meats being the first items, which were options of fried chicken, baked chicken, meat loaf and liver. Next were two kinds of gravy, followed by sides of steamed rice, green beans, lima beans, collard greens, Macaroni and Cheese, candied yams and cabbage. This was followed by corn bread, Peach cobbler, Red velvet cake and lemon pound cake. Tonya stood admiring the spread that was fit for a king.

"What would you like today?" a lady behind the counter asked. She stood with a hurried look of her face as Tonya tried to decide what she wanted to eat.

"So many choices, I can't decide."

The server was not amused by Tonya's indecisiveness. She looked over her glasses and gave Tonya a warning glance.

Tonya quickly selected baked chicken and moved on to the next server for her sides and dessert. No one could make Mac-N-Cheese like Sister White, but she'd have to see how this place stacked up to Sister White's prize dish.

Elder Lacey chose a table with three chairs that was near the back of the small room. He needed some privacy talk to his daughter. He needed to get to the bottom of what was going with Tonya and Keith. The table cloth was of fall leaves with a gold back ground. A silver napkin holder was placed in the center of the table. A single artificial rose in a small vase sat on the right side and a salt and pepper shakers sat on the opposite side.

"Does this have anything to do with your living with Carmen?" he asked, pointing at Tonya's battered face as the three took seats at the table. Although Tonya tried to disguise her bruises with makeup, she still couldn't hide the swollen lip and puffy eyes. She knew that her father would not overlook that fact.

"Yes, sir." Tonya suddenly felt like a ten-year-old who had done something wrong and was awaiting punishment.

"Why don't you tell me what happened?"

"I…don't know where to start."

"Try the beginning," Elder Lacey said in a stern voice, as he interlaced his fingers and placed them on the table, giving Tonya his undivided attention.

He sat quietly as she recapped the frightful evening when she had revealed her health status to Keith. Elder Lacey sat forward at the mention of HIV, as if he would fall from his chair. Carmen grabbed her shocked father's arm in an attempt to steady him. Tonya never had seen him look so frail and vulnerable. The blood had drained from his face, and he looked ill. It was as if he were crumbling before her eyes.

The trio sat in silence as Elder Lacey regained his composure. He was at a loss for words. He closed his eyes and whispered a silent prayer. He quickly placed his trembling hands in his lap; they felt like deadweight. He wanted to go and find Keith and do some serious damage to him. He didn't condone men putting their hands on women, but he especially didn't condone it when it concerned his two daughters. He clenched and unclenched his fist as he thought about using his hands to rectify the damage done to his daughter. Although he'd feel much better after beating the snot out of Keith, he knew that it would solve nothing. He had raised his daughters to be strong women, who spoke their mind and walked in their individual belief. The difference between his two daughters is Tonya has a soft heart and always excused away other people's faults. Carmen was the opposite of her older sister. Carmen would challenge a bull frog sitting on his own lily pad if given the chance. She reminded him of a much younger him in the sense that she was very outspoken and opinionated. Tonya, much like Bethany, was always meek mannered, but it was often mistaken for weakness until they showed you just how strong they really were.

Looking at the buffet of food sitting before them order, no one seemed to have much of an appetite. She knew that her father hated wasting food, but she was suddenly no longer hungry.

Tonya never had been the type of person to doubt her faith, but her life had changed so drastically. "What did I do to cause this to come upon me?" she asked, as the tears became small puddles on the table, as if signifying the shedding of her belief system as well as her father's lifelong teachings. She looked to Elder Lacey for guidance. He always had been the rock of the family, and being a man of God, he'd surely have a word for her.

He placed his hands on the table with both palms up; Tonya and Carmen each placed a hand in his. The trio prayed. Elder Lacey asked God to guide him in dealing with their present situation. He then looked at his eldest daughter and smiled.

"Sweetheart, the day your mother gave birth to you was one of the happiest days of my life," he said. "If ever I doubted the Lord existed, that day removed all doubt, because I knew at that moment that he was smiling down on me. Even as a child, you were filled with so much love, laughter, and life. Nothing can change the love I have for you. I could never be ashamed of you, because you've always made me so proud of you. You're a blessing from God. God knew Bethany wouldn't be here forever, so he gave me the two of you. I got double for my trouble!"

Beaming with pride as he looked at his daughters, Elder Lacey counted his blessings.

"We were so blessed to have you two girls, so hold your heads up and know you're loved, and we'll get through this awful tribulation."

Tears had formed behind Elder Lacey's eyes as he spoke to his daughters. Carmen and Tonya couldn't maintain their composure as they held hands and cried openly as their father expressed his love for them. A father's love could heal a multitude of aches and pain.

Carmen looked at the veggie plate that sat before her and frowned.

"What's wrong? Is there something wrong with your food?" Tonya asked her.

"No, I just got my appetite back and realized I'm going to need some meat to go along with these vegetables."

"Yes, I think we've allregained our appetites," Tonya said, laughing at Carmen, who was known for her hearty appetite.

22

Checking out the dark clouds overhead, Tonya could smell the approaching rain as she exited her office building. She raced to her car and jumped in as the first drop of rain hit the hood of her car. Trying to beat the rain was useless as the quarter-size droplets hit her windshield. She turned on the wipers and decelerated as she drove through the hazardous weather. It was only four thirty, but the sky already had gotten dark. Cars zipped past her, as drivers blared their horns and pointed their middle fingers at her to show their annoyance as she drove at a snail's pace. She was glad she couldn't hear the insults that flew from their mouths as they glared at her.

—⁓—

"You drive your car, and I'll drive mine!" she yelled, as a car swerved around her.

Another car crossed into her lane rather closely as a second car pulled up close to her on her left. She jerked the wheel to the right and braked to avoid collision, which resulted in her losing control of the vehicle. The tires slid across the wet asphalt. She gripped the wheel tightly, hoping to regain control, but her panic sent her car into a tailspin.

"Jesus! Oh, Lord!" she screamed, as her car spun around before coming to a rest.

With her head pressed against the steering wheel, Tonya tried to process the event. The thought of the near accident shook her up and put her nerves on edge. She considered calling someone to come pick her up, but leaving her car on the interstate wasn't an option.

As she sat in her car on the side of the highway, her head pounded as she tried to make sense of what had just occurred. She'd been experiencing frequent headaches and dizzy spells for the past three weeks. She knew they were a result of her high blood pressure or, as the doctor called it, pregnancy-induced hypertension. She had watched her sodium intake, but how could she eliminate salt from her diet when everything was cooked in it or coated in it? She had cut back on canned, packaged, and processed foods as instructed, but even that didn't seem to do the trick. Her last blood-pressure reading during her obstetric appointment was a disconcerting 170 over 110. At the time she didn't feel lightheaded and had no idea that her blood pressure was even elevated. She was sure she'd have some sort of warning if her blood pressure were that high. Besides the headaches and dizzy spells, Tonya was experiencing blurred vision. She wondered which of those three had contributed to her accident.

Driving in the torrential rain would be a battle, but she'd have to brave the weather rather than leave her car behind. Condensation covered the windows as she peered out to see traffic passing her. She fumbled with the defrost button, the AC, and the heater, as the cold air increased the thick condensation and the heater made her uncomfortably hot. She settled for warm air and turned it up as high as she could to eliminate the condensation from her windows.

She sat and prayed for a safe drive home. *I'll sit and wait a minute until it eases up before I get back into that crazy traffic*, she thought.

Tonya nervously laughed as she reflected on the advice Sister Peggy's had given her a few years ago. "When you can't do no more, just stand der and watch God." She was attempting to quote gospel music singer and minister Donnie McClurkin. "After you done all you can, you just stand." Tonya had gotten the gist. At this moment she decided to take that same advice and sit and wait.

As the downpour became less threatening, Tonya eased back into traffic.

When she arrived at Carmen's house and got out of the car, she was soaked to the bone. Not wanting to upset her sister, she decided not to mention the near accident. As she opened the front door and stepped inside, she welcomed the warmth of Carmen's home. She smelled food cooking in the kitchen, which instantly made her hungry.

"It's raining cats and dogs out there," Carmen said.

"Tell me about it. I think I brought in a few strays this way. I've got to get out of these wet clothes. I've had a hard day trying to finish the monthly report for work."

"Well, dry off and relax. Dinner should be ready soon."

Carmen made Tonya's favorite meal, chicken Alfredo with fettuccini. She had found a recipe that was low in sodium, which Tonya needed. She also had used fresh boneless, skinless chicken breasts; fat-free reduced-sodium chicken broth; and garlic powder, which gave her the benefits of a healthy fat-and-cholesterol-reduced meal.

After the delicious meal, Tonya sat on the couch and elevated her swollen feet. Even though she tried to maintain a healthy diet and watched her sodium intake, her extremities seemed to have a mind of their own.

Carmen sat at the computer, typing and looking and intently looking at the screen.

"What are you doing?" Tonya asked.

"Chatting. There are some really interesting people out there in cyberspace."

"Don't mess around and catch yourself a predator," Tonya joked.

"Very funny! I'm actually chatting with people in an HIV chat room."

"Are you serious?" Tonya asked, jumping up from the couch.

"Come on. Let me show you."

Carmen showed Tonya the different chat rooms she had visited, where people shared their personal experiences with the disease.

"They don't mind talking about it in the open?" Tonya asked.

"Some don't. Some have even posted their pictures."

Together they sat at the computer surfing the Internet. Carmen showed Tonya the different educational sites that listed statistics, case studies, and facts about the virus and disease.

"Call me naive, but I never knew all this was out there," Tonya said excitedly.

"That's not half of what's available. Let's look at the CDC website. It has a mother lode of information," Carmen said, referring to the Centers for Disease Control site.

After chatting with a few people online, Tonya felt a connection. No longer was she by herself; in fact there were thousands of people like her, and they weren't afraid to tell their stories. They even encouraged her when they themselves were in similar or worse situations. Tonya felt comfortable chatting in the comfort of Carmen's home, but didn't feel she could share her HIV status with those she knew personally—not even Sister Peggy.

She spent hours online. She enjoyed having the opportunity to meet people who had walked in her shoes and had survived. One man shared his story of having been infected for more fifteen years; Tonya never thought anyone with HIV could live that long.

"I guess people with money can live longer than the average person, huh?" Tonya asked the person on the other side of her computer screen.

"What does that mean?" he typed.

"You know, people like Magic Johnson. He's still alive because he has millions of dollars."

"Well, I wouldn't say that. Liberace had money, and I'm sure a lot of people would give everything they owned if it would keep them healthy. It's up to us to work at keeping ourselves healthy and infection free."

Tonya sat back and processed the thought of money having very little to do with living longer with HIV. She remembered Rock Hudson and how he'd had money as well, but he had died in the mid-1980s, when AIDS was still thought of as a gay disease. She'd never felt more ignorant than she did at this moment. How could she have thought that anyone wouldn't give his or her last dime to find a cure or at least a reliable treatment for the disease?

In June 1982 an NBC News reporter had reported on what was described as a mysterious disease that seemed to primarily strike homosexual men and was thought to be a rare cancer. During that time it was called Gay-Related Immune Deficiency (GRID), but doctors and researchers quickly realized it could affect anyone.

Tonya was very impressed with one man who was very open about his struggle with AIDS, sharing in the chat room how he contended with multiple co-infections such as hepatitis C and herpes, and multiple physical debilitating factors as the disease took its toll on his body. Tonya's heart sank as she thought about progressing to such a state. She was always tired, but she thought her pregnancy was the culprit.

After talking to the group, she realized she wasn't the only one experiencing bouts of nausea, vomiting, diarrhea, headaches, and dizziness. She felt extremely tired all the time as well, but she'd attributed these issues to being normal symptoms of pregnancy. It was difficult to distinguish pregnancy from the growing symptoms of HIV.

The group compared war stories about their battles with having to take multiple pills. One person had to take a dozen or more pills a day, while others said theyhad to take as few as six, with many being combination pills. The main issue that repeated itself was the importance of storing the medication properly and taking it with food, or a high-fat snack, even when you didn't have an appetite. They found that doing so minimized the side effects of the medications.

Tonya ended her chat session with a promise to return often, as it was a new source of support for her. No one wants to feel as if he or she is the only person with a problem or disease, especially one of this magnitude. She most certainly would be back.

23

Keith's cell phone blasted his favorite song, which he'd downloaded as his ringtone, "B.U.D.D.Y." by Musiq Soulchild. He had designated the song as his anthem. Recognizing the number, he frowned and answered the phone with anger and frustration oozing from his voice. "Shayla, what do you want? I told you—"

An unfamiliar voice cut him off midsentence.

"K.J?"

The voice definitely wasn't Shayla, and he didn't recognize it.

"Yeah, this is K.J. Who's this?"

"This is Latasha, Shayla's sister."

He remembered Shayla's younger sister. He had been nice to the girl and had even had a few laughs with her but why was she calling him?

"Shayla wanted me to let you know she's sorry for not being able to tell you herself, but you need to get tested."

Keith looked at the phone in disbelief. "What? Tested for what? Where is she? Put her on the phone!"

Silence.

"Hello?" Keith hear sniffling on the other end. The girl was crying.

"K.J., Shayla died last week. The doctors said it was from complications of AIDS; she caught pneumonia and couldn't fight it. She wanted to tell you herself, but you wouldn't accept her calls. She gave me a list of names and numbers and made me promise to tell you and others she might have infected."

Keith couldn't believe his ears. *AIDS? List of names? How could she not tell me and continue to sleep with me? Why send her sister to do her dirty work by having her tell me news of this caliber? How could she do such a thing?*

"K.J, are you still there?"

"Uh, yeah, I'm here. So exactly how long did she know about this?"

"Oh, she knew for quite some time. She contracted the virus in high school, but that never stopped her."

Keith became furious. "High school! That's more a decade ago, long before I met her. How could she?"

"K.J., my family tried to tell Shayla not to sleep around, but her motto was, 'I ain't dead yet!' She just wanted to enjoy her life."

"And take out as many people as she could before she left?" Keith yelled into the phone. "You people are sick. How could you look me in the face and not say a word?" Tears welled in his eyes as he thought of dying before his time. "You sick, twisted...She'd better be glad she's dead, because I'd kill her myself!"

A sick feeling came over him. His stomach felt as if it were hollow yet full of rocks at the same time. A sense of doom overcame his as the thought of what Latasha was saying became his truth.

Deep inside, however, he knew he couldn't blame Latasha or Shayla; he was the one who had stepped outside of his marriage.

"K.J., I'm sorry, but she was my sister, and I didn't owe you a thing. I have enough on my plate. I have to raise her son, who's also sick. This child no longer has a mother, and his dad is locked up for life. Just go get tested." Latasha hung up the phone.

Keith hadn't gotten tested when Tonya had first broken the news to him four months ago that she was HIV positive. There was no need to get tested because he wasn't sick. He didn't need an HIV test to tell him that. He'd read as much as he could stand about the virus. He read about the flulike symptoms people have and how the virus progress. He hadn't experienced any of those symptoms—no nausea, vomiting, diarrhea, or weight loss. He was perfectly healthy. He still ran five miles every day, worked out at the gym regularly, and played basketball with the fellows when he could.

The one thing that bothered him was the fact that he'd thought his wife had acquired the virus from sleeping around, when he had been to blame. He hadn't slept with her after she'd told him she was HIV positive, so he was fairly certain he wasn't infected.

Keith stood still with the phone in his hand, dazed and lost, wondering how many more guys Latasha had to call with this dreadful news, and how on earth he could tell Tonya. *Oh, God,* he thought. *What about my wife and our unborn child? I gave them both a death sentence.* Keith sobbed as he dropped to his knees in the middle of the sidewalk. Pedestrians walked around him, staring and whispering as they passed him on the street, probably taking him for a crazed person or a homeless man looking for a handout. Unable to will his shaking legs to stand, he sat crumpled on the ground. He hated Shayla and everything she represented. He was quickly reminded of the warning Brian had given him months ago when he'd seen Shayla profiling on the blue Mustang—"Don't even think about it. That horse is too wild, and I don't mean the car." Keith cursed the day he had met Shayla and the day she was born.

He had lost all sense of time from the moment he'd received the call from Latasha. He was confused and disoriented, feeling numb and lost, with no idea where he was, until a young woman stood before him with his cell phone in her hand.

"Sir, I think you dropped this. Are you all right?"

Do I look like I'm all right? Keith thought. *I'm a murderer!*

The young lady paused, as if waiting for a response, then placed the phone in Keith's hand. With a look of pity, she walked away, muttering, "Lord, bless his soul."

Rage erupted from Keith as his senses returned. *How could Shayla do this to me? AIDS? Only gays, crackheads, and junkies get that disease—oh, yeah, and people like Shayla!* Brian's warning echoed in his head like a scratched record, *Don't even think about it. That horse is too wild, and I don't mean the car.* Keith thought about the constant warnings he'd gotten from Brian and Jerry and how he'd ignored them. His friends had practically begged him to leave Shayla alone, especially after they'd found about their affair. Keith had been too infatuated to listen to anything that would shine a negative light on Shayla. He should have known she was too good to be true.

They probably would cut him loose when they found out that he didn't listen to them but had gone behind their back and continued the affair and now probably had ended up acquiring the dreaded disease. "Man, I was so wrong for accusing Tonya," Keith mumbled, as he staggered to his feet, trying to pull himself together. He wanted to kick himself for not listening to his friends in the first place and putting his life and Tonya's in jeopardy. *God, how am I supposed to tell Tonya?* he thought. *Baby, I've got some bad news. I think I gave you HIV.* Keith rehearsed his lines in his mind as he tried to collect himself and prepare for the talk he'd inevitably have to have with his estranged pregnant wife. But first he'd better get tested himself.

Hoping against all odds, Keith prayed that it was just a hoax and that Shayla hadn't given him HIV. Perhaps it was just a coincidence that his wife had ended up with the same thing.

Only a fool would believe that, he told himself.

After the long wait at the doctor's office, since he didn't have an appointment, Keith was finally called in to be seen by Dr. Gipson. He and his wife had the same doctor, which made it easier for both of them when they had appointments the same day. Keith hardly ever went to the doctor, only once or twice a year during the winter, when he inevitably got the flu or a sinus infection. He considered himself a healthy person. He ran a mile and a half every morning, limited his meat intake, and drank alcohol only occasionally. He was what most people call a social drinker, but Tonya preferred that he not drink at all.

The doctor, being familiar with his medical history, asked him a list of questions regarding whether he had symptoms of nausea, vomiting, diarrhea, and fatigue. Keith knew where he was going with this—no, he didn't feel sick.

"I spoke with your wife, and she told me you had refused to get tested because you didn't feel sick. Can you tell me why you're coming in now?"

"I found out an ex-girlfriend died from AIDS," Keith said.

"I'm sorry to hear that. Well, it's a good decision for you to get tested."

"I need to know if I was the one who gave it to my wife. I've got to know, Doc."

"I should have your test results when you come back for your next appointment. I'll have the test done today. We'll discuss the results on your follow-up visit."

"Thanks, Doctor. I just need to know."

Dr. Gipson gave Keith a full physical and took blood samples. The receptionist gave him an appointment to return to his office in three weeks, which was the soonest appointment available.

Three weeks! he thought. *How am I supposed to get through the next three weeks?* Keith pleaded with the receptionist to see if she could book him sooner.

"I'm sorry, sir, but that's the earliest date available."

"I guess I have no choice but to keep that appointment." Keith sighed deeply, took the appointment card from the receptionist, and put it in his wallet.

Walking away, Keith felt dejected. He couldn't possibly survive the next three weeks not knowing whether he was infected. Looking around the waiting room, he wondered how many of those sitting in there had HIV or AIDS. *Maybe that skinny, sickly-looking woman, or is it that old dude with the Jheri curl? Well, he's got to be sick to wear that tired hairdo, if nothing else,* Keith thought, as he left the doctor's office.

Feeling anxious and with time on his hands, Keith went to Rob's Place for a couple of beers. He needed to pass the time and alleviate his fears. Sitting at the bar was Tony, a guy he'd gone to high school with, and Darlene, a round-the-way girl who frequented the area. Tony spotted Keith and beckoned him over.

"Hey, man. Long time, no see!"

"Yeah, I know."

"Where you been keeping yo'self?" Tony asked with a slur.

"Working, keeping busy, you know." Keith wondered how long Tony had been sitting at the bar and just how much he had consumed. Even though the lighting in the bar was dim, he could see Tony's eyes were bloodshot and glassy.

"Good for you. Just keep on keeping on. I'll be right back." He stood up and stumbled, grabbing the stool he'd been sitting on to steady himself. Keith snatched him by the arm and helped him gain his balance. He held on to the man before deciding he could stand on his own. Tony stood up straight, brushed away some invisible lint from his shirt, and tilted his head in pride before moving away from the barstool. Keith watched him stagger to the rear of the bar toward the bathroom, swaying back and forth like a pendulum.

"Hey, handsome," a female voice yelled over the loud crooning of Alicia Keys's "A Woman's Worth," which was playing on the jukebox. No need to turn around—he knew Darlene was talking to him. He could smell the foul odor of stale cigarettes and booze that radiated from her unclean body as she slid next to him. The sight of Darlene irritated him, and the thought of her pushing up on him repulsed him.

"Shouldn't you be at home with your kids?" he asked her. "What are you up to now? Six?"

"It's none of your damn business how many children I got! Who made you my daddy?"

"Darlene, why don't you slither right back over there. Better yet, go change your babies' diapers and feed them. Go home and be a mother!"

"K.J., you trying to act like you're more than everybody else since you got a good job, but you ain't no better than me!" she shouted. "I knew you before you had that job. I knew you when you was just a wannabe baller!"

Darlene and Keith had gone to the same high school, but she had dropped out in the tenth grade to become a mother to her first child and had babies every two to three years since. Eventually she started smoking crack cocaine and drinking on a regular basis, which is what she bought with her children's welfare money. She sold her food stamps for crack, leaving her children to fend for themselves. She now lived with her mother, who took care of her children. Darlene spent most of her time at either Rob's Place, a crack house, or some pay-by-the-hour motel. She had been a fairly attractive girl in high school, but she lived a fast life. Now she looked nothing like the girl Keith once knew. Her teeth were decayed; she was missing a couple of molars; and her hair was matted to her scalp. She wore clothes that looked like something someone had thrown out or given to the Salvation Army. Her children were in better shape, only due to Darlene's mother being a caring woman who was dedicated to her grandchildren.

Shaking his head, Keith pitied her children. As he ordered his drink of Rémy, he heard Darlene whisper to T-Bone, the bartender, "Make that two. My friend here is buying."

"Any drink you enjoy will be bought by you or some unlucky trick who happens your way, but it won't be me. Go home and take care of your babies!"

Offended by Keith's rejection, Darlene snatched her handbag off the bar and headed out the door, yelling over her shoulder, "K.J., you're still a louse!"

"Another case of the pot calling the kettle black," Keith mumbled.

T-Bone laughed as they watched her leave. "Man, pay Darlene no mind. She'll be right back in here in the next twenty minutes and forget you were ever here. That girl's mind is gone!"

"That bad, huh?"

"This is a good day. She recognized you. Most days she don't even know her own kids. She's been in and out of jail and the nuthouse, but what she needs is a good detox center."

"How many kids is she' up to now?"

"Seven. And the last three are crack babies."

"What happened to her?" Keith asked.

"The streets happened to her."

24

Trying to hide her face in embarrassment, Tonya arrived forty-five minutes earlier than usual in an attempt to avoid the office whispers. She felt self-conscious about her newly swollen lip. But no matter how hard she tried to avoid nosy Mary and her gossiping tongue, it was short-lived.

Mary slowly approached her and stood over her desk. She looked at Tonya, leaned forward, and pointed her crooked finger in her face. "Maybe a little Abreva wouldn't hurt. It works wonders on fever blisters."

Tonya was mortified at the thought of anyone noticing her inflamed lips. How could Mary be so bold? She'd had the audacity to come right out and let it be known that she knew she'd contracted herpes.

"Oh, I'm sure it'll go down," Tonya told her. "It's the stress of pregnancy, I'm sure."

"Well, I had a baby, and I didn't have that kind of stress." Mary smirked as Tonya turned her head to hide her face.

Tonya wasn't amused. "Well, by the looks of things, Mary, you might want to lose a bit of your baby fat."

Mary's jaw went slack.

Tonya's phone rang, as if on cue. "Thanks, Mary. Gotta get this line." Tonya picked up the line and left Mary standing gawking before her.

She decided to make a run to the drugstore on her lunch break. *I'll try anything once*, she thought. She had to pick up her prescription of Diflucan anyway.

How did I get to this point? she wondered, as she waited in line at the pharmacy.

The pharmacist, a dark-complexioned, chubby-faced young man, approached her. He looked at her with a half-smile, or so Tonya thought. Her imagination began to play tricks on her as she scanned the store.

Does he know I have HIV? she wondered. The man smiled as he handed her the bag with her prescription. *Is he laughing in my face?* Shaking her head, Tonya mumbled, "Get it together, girl."

"Mrs. Paris, here's your prescription. Drink plenty of water when taking this medication. Don't consume alcohol while taking it, and make sure you take the medication as directed. Please read the literature enclosed, and call your doctor if you experience any of the potential side effects listed. Do you have any questions?"

Handling the white bag made her nervous and paranoid, as if everyone in the pharmacy knew what it contained. "No, thank you." Tonya paid for her medication, along with tube of Abreva, and quickly exited the pharmacy.

A few days later, during one of her visits to Dr. Thomas Smith, her obstetrician, a blood culture was drawn. During her next visit, she learned she was positive for herpes simplex and candidiasis, a fungal infection. This latest diagnosis was just one more blow to her already devastated self-worth, and she lamented over the changes in her body. She had been faithful in taking her medications, but even so, she had contracted an infection. Dr. Smith already had warned her about keeping her T-cell count above two hundred and mentioned a long list of opportunistic infections she might contract; herpes and candidiasis were two of those dreaded infections.

At first Tonya had thought she just had a bad yeast infection. She had read that pregnant women often got yeast infections, but she wasn't just another woman carrying a baby. She was a pregnant woman who had been diagnosed with HIV. Until recently, given the rapid change in her health and the recurrent episodes of infections, she no longer had HIV but was now a carrier of AIDS.

Tonya began to cry; it seemed as if this nightmare would never end. Dr. Smith tried to explain the disease process to her, but she was too overwhelmed to grasp all the details. What did all this mean? CD4 count and percentages, T-helper cells, viral load test—it was just too much. Feeling a headache coming on, she was too tired to comprehend all the complicated information. She felt as if an atomic bomb had hit her. She couldn't retain the slightest bit of information at that moment. All she knew was that the doctor had told her that her CD4 level had dropped below two, and she had acquired those two opportunistic infections, and now she had AIDS. Her already compromised immune system along with her pregnancy was too much for her to bear.

Once she was able to process this news, it was devastating. Tonya was in total turmoil. She wondered how long she had to live and how she'd be able to raise her child while she was slowly dying.

"After you treat this infection, and my level goes back up to an acceptable number, will I no longer have AIDS?" Tonya said, hoping for a positive answer.

"Well, Mrs. Paris, I'm just your obstetrician. Dr. Gipson will treat you for your medical condition. But be aware that there isn't a cure for AIDS, and once you've been diagnosed with the disease, you'll always carry that diagnosis. The treatment of any infections as well as the elevation of your CD4 level won't indicate a cure, but it will mean you've been treated successfully for that particular infection."

"Why wasn't I diagnosed with AIDS before this?"

"Well, the introduction of the infection, along with the drop in your T-cells, has caused you to meet the criteria for AIDS set by the CDC."

"What about my baby?"

"Your baby will be tested when he's a little older. Because he carries your antibodies, he could test positive at birth, but by the age of eighteen months, he'll have developed his own antibodies and may be able to fight off the infection."

Feeling better about keeping her baby, Tonya felt reassured that things would work out. Now if she could just get rid of this darn yeast infection and the fever blisters that lined her lips. People often shied away from her when they looked at her mouth. "This must be how lepers felt," Tonya muttered.

Pulling into a parking space at church, Tonya felt a tightening in her chest and rubbed her chest with the palm of her hand. Carmen looked over at her sister, who wore a pained expression.

"Are you all right?" she asked with concern in her voice.

"Must be my lunch coming back to visit me."

"What did you eat? Beans again?"

"No, I had a chili dog. I guess it's just as bad, huh?" Tonya asked, before reaching into her purse and popping a couple of TUMS into her mouth. She'd been taking so many TUMS lately that she thought about buying stock in the company.

"Don't worry about dinner. I'm cooking my famous salmon tonight!"

"I really don't want to talk about your cooking right now," Tonya chided Carmen, as she opened the car door. Tonya loved her sister's baked lemon-pepper salmon, but the thought of food right was making her stomach do flips.

Tonya slowly got out of the car and made their way up the church steps. With each step she took, she heard herself wheezing. She didn't know how she could tolerate the cold weather or her church activities any longer. The short walk left her tired and lightheaded. Pausing at the top of the steps, she leaned against the door.

"Are you OK?" Carmen asked, her grabbing her sister's hand.

"Just a little winded. I'm carrying extra weight here." Tonya smiled as she patted her growing belly.

"OK. Just make sure you let me know if you begin to feel sick. We don't need you falling out all over the place."

"I'm fine. I just needed to get my bearings."

Unsure whether Tonya was being truthful, Carmen decided to keep an eye on her.

During choir rehearsal Tonya had to sit down in the middle of a song because her breath was coming in short gasps. She couldn't hold her notes as long as she used to, and she was having increased episodes of syncope.

"Tonya, are you OK? Why don't you drink a little water? It'll make you feel better," Carmen suggested, handing Tonya a bottle of water.

"I've been so tired lately. These spells come and go. I'll be all right."

Choir rehearsal lasted longer than usual, since the choir hadn't been able to meet as often because the choir director, Daryl, and his wife recently had welcomed their third child. He was always bothered with those rug rats of his, Daryl Jr. ("D.J.") and Keon. They were ages four and five respectively and had the energy of six children. One day Daryl had to stop rehearsal so many times to chastise his boys that the choir did more standing and waiting instead of singing. Finally Sister Peggy came upstairs from her office and took the boys to the room where they held Sunday school. The choir was able to practice for two whole hours without interruptions.

During another rehearsal, Deacon Frazier walked in while the boys were there and saw them jumping in the pews, running up and down the aisles and banging on the drums. He slowly walked over to D.J. with his hand behind his back, leaned over, and whispered into the little boy's ear. The boy's eyes grew wide as he listened intently to the deacon. D.J. immediately dropped his head and slowly walked over and sat in the front-row pew. Whatever Deacon Frazier had said quieted him down for the rest of the practice. Keon quickly fell silent at the mere sight of Deacon Frazier, so there was no need for the deacon to approach him. He took a seat next to his brother in the pew, neither boy uttering a word.

One of the choir members whispered loud enough for a few of the others to hear, "Deacon Frazier knows how to put the fear of God in you!" This was followed by laughter from those in earshot but a frown from Daryl. The boys didn't attend rehearsals as often after that.

25

Carmen raced down the stairway to her office parking lot, wanting to take two steps at a time but knowing she'd fall flat on her face. Speed-walking would have to do. She jumped in her car and backed up without taking a second look, almost colliding with Dale, a maintenance worker. She drove off in such a hurry that she didn't see her coworker Brooke waving good-bye to her from the garage stairway. She was too busy trying to keep her scheduled appointment with her girlfriends from college. She was excited to see her friends again, especially since the women had parted ways shortly after graduation. Although they'd managed to keep in touch by phone long distance, it wasn't the same as hanging out in person. The five o'clock traffic was hectic as usual, and her patience was as thin as a razor. She checked her watch for the third time in the last ten minutes. She knew that trying to get there on time would be an almost impossible task. Carmen blew a lungful of air in frustration as she came to a stop at the traffic light. *Must every light turn red when I approach?* she wondered. After fumbling in her purse for her cell phone, she called her friend Cheryl.

Cheryl was the mother figure of the group, always precise about managing time andextremely detailed. The women referred to her as "Mother Hen," as she always kept the women in line. Sometimes her motherly advice made the other girls angry, but they appreciated her wisdom, which was beyond her years. Cheryl never could relax and just have a good time; she always had to be the voice of reason. One good thing about hanging out with Cheryl was that the women always had a designated driver.

"Hey, running late," Carmen told her. "This traffic is jacked up!"

"You're not the only one running late. Denise got stuck with her wedding planner and called to say she's on her way as well."

"Where's Jocelyn?"'

"She's here, forever texting someone or talking on her cell."

The women always laughed at Jocelyn's obsession with her cell phone. They often joked that if she ever lost her phone, she'd lose her mind.

"You know that thing is going to get embedded in her skull if she doesn't stay off it," Cheryl said, loud enough for Jocelyn to hear.

"Well, I'll see you whenever I can get through this parade of traffic."

"Take your time and be safe."

Carmen tapped her finger on the steering wheel as traffic crawled along the interstate. Driving from the outskirts of the city tt o the downtown area, where they had reserved a suite at the Embassy Hotel, would be a doozy. She wouldn't arrive at her destination anytime soon. Checking her watch again, she frowned. Only five minutes had passed since she had ended her call with Cheryl. No one else seemed to mind that traffic wasn't moving. She glanced at the driver to her left, who showed no sign of irritation; in fact he was bobbing his head and singing along to whatever was playing on the radio. Carmen turned on her stereo, selected a CD, adjusted her sunglasses, and listened to the sensual sound of Kevon Edmonds to ease her wrecked nerves. He definitely would keep her mind off the slow-moving traffic.

After an irritating hour-long drive that normally took thirty-five minutes, Carmen finally pulled up to the hotel to meet up with her friends. She was excited to see them after such a long separation. The four women had made plans to reunite several times over the past year, something always seemed to stand in their way. After hugging one another and checking out how each had changed over the few years they'd been apart, the women sat down catch up on their lives over glasses of wine. The suite was large enough to accommodate all four women. There were two king sized beds in each rooms. The overlook from balcony was a beautiful view of the city below. The patio door was opened and a welcoming cool breeze penetrated the room. A vase of freshly cut orchids sat on a dining table near the open patio door. The sweet smell filled the room with a gentle tease. Carmen excitedly embraced the women as she entered the suite. The women giggled and squealed as they hugged each other. She couldn't believe Cheryl had cut her hair. She'd always worn her hair long, but now she wore it in a short pageboy style. She'd also gained about fifteen pounds, but it looked good on her. She was much too small in college and was often teased about resembling a Q-Tip, with her full head of hair and small frame. Denise had changed very little. She was probably the same size she was in college. She wore more makeup than she did back then, but she was as pretty as ever, with her deep-brown oval eyes that turned up at the corner, giving her the appearance of an Asian woman. Jocelyn hadn't changed one iota and was just as busy and scattered as she had been in college. Looking at Jocelyn, who was texting as she talked to Denise, Carmen smirked. *Some things never change*, she thought. Jocelyn had not physically changed much over the years either. She was a petite 5'6 with beautiful brown eyes, which she hid behind hazel contacts. She had a small red birthmark between her eyebrows, which resembled the traditional red dot worn by Indian woman that symbolize that they are married. She kept her lean figure that she developed while playing volley ball in high school. Her long brown shoulder length hair was worn in loose curls. The false lashes she wore gave her an air of being snooty, as the lashes turned upward. She was naturally a beautiful girl, who didn't need a lot of makeup, but she slathered it on anyway. She loved the attention.

The reunion had brought them back from jobs, marriage, and traveling. Cheryl, a dental hygienist, had come back home to get married and start a family after college. Her inability to have children despite using fertility drugs had kept her feeling stressed. The remaining three women were still single, but Denise was engaged and planning a wedding, which kept her busy and out of the loop. She worked as an accountant. She was good with numbers but always had poor judgment when it came to men. Jocelyn, the youngest of the group, was still trying to find herself. She had changed careers twice since graduation. Jocelyn loved to hear herself talk. She'd probably get to know herself better if she spent more time with herself and off that darn cell phone. Cheryl ordered sandwiches and salads for the women while they got caught up on what was happening in their lives. As the women sat around the dining-room table, sharing photos of their loved ones, Carmen thought about Tonya and how her life had drastically changed. Taking this time to discuss what was weighing heavily on her mind, she introduced the topic. She'd been thinking about it ever since Melody, a coworker, had revealed to her that her boyfriend recently had confessed to being attracted to both men and women but denied being gay. He had told Melody he didn't feel gay, because he didn't have the urge to dress like a woman or act feminine, and he sure didn't walk like a gay man, but he still found himself looking at men in a sexual manner.

"What do you think about DL brothers?" Carmen said, referring to "down-low brothers," the name given to supposedly straight men who sleep with other men.

Jocelyn scrunched her face and turned her lip up. "It's disgusting! They should just man up to what they really are!" she blurted out, as she checked her cell phone for an incoming call.

"Did you hear the Strawberry Letter on Steve Harvey's *Morning Show* about the man who was dating the preacher and the deacon in the same church?" Denise asked.

"Are you kidding?" Jocelyn asked, flipping open her phone to answer the call.

"I wish," Denise said. "The man said that both men were secretly taking care of him financially and physically, if you get my drift."

"In the church?" Carmen asked in amazement.

Denise nodded. "In the church."

"Do we revere nothing anymore?"

"Why not just man up and say 'I'm gay,' instead of playing the role of a straight man?" Denise said.

"I can't right now, but I'll call you later," Jocelyn spoke into the phone. The women looked annoyed as she carried on a separate conversation.

"They don't believe they're gay or bisexual. In their minds they're straight but have sex with men," Denise continued.

"Now that's some prison thinking for you!" Cheryl added.

"Well, that's one form of thinking that they need to send back to Cell Block H," Carmen said.

"Wait, what did I miss?" Jocelyn said, as she ended her phone call.

"You wouldn't have missed a word if you weren't so involved in that phone call," Cheryl chastised her. "We're right in the middle of a discussion."

"Sorry," Jocelyn said sheepishly, hunching her shoulders and taking a seat next to Denise.

Sensing an opportunity, Carmen posed her loaded question. "Do you think that's why so many black women are getting HIV, because our men are straddling the fence?"

"I believe that's one of the reasons," Jocelyn said.

"They need to change it from 'down-low brothers' to 'don't lie brothers' or 'stop spreading the disease brothers,' or better yet just 'low-down brothers,' " Denise chimed in.

The women gave high-fives all around.

"That's why our women are dying of AIDS. Those men can't make up their minds one way or the other, so they keep up appearances to look good for society," Cheryl said.

"That's deep but true," Denise added.

"Do you remember that guy from New York who gave dozens of women HIV in the early nineties?" Jocelyn asked.

"Who can forget him!" Cheryl said. "He exposed fifty or more women and young girls to HIV before they locked him up."

"They didn't give him enough time if you ask me. What's four to twelve years when people lives are at stake?" Jocelyn said.

"Most drug dealers get three to five for selling drugs, and serial killers get life without the possibility of parole, or the death penalty, and so should he." Cheryl was usually high-strung when it came to the justice system. She was known for quoting the saying, "There no justice—just us."

"He got off easy if you ask me," Carmen added. "What happens when he gets out of prison? Who will protect unsuspecting women? He's still a young man."

"He'll probably get swept under the carpet, until he infects another twenty or thirty women." Jocelyn became animated, flinging her arms while trying to make her point.

"Dating is so scary today," Carmen said. "You don't know what you're getting, a gay man or an infected one. I guess you need a gaydar in one hand and an HIV test in the other."

"Amen to that!" Jocelyn and Cheryl said.

Denise, who had suddenly gotten quiet, simply nodded. She had her own personal fears to contend with, since her brother Thomas had been discharged from the military after being diagnosed with AIDS. Thomas was sent home to be treated, but things didn't look promising for him. He denied being sick and refused treatment out of fear of anyone finding out about his illness. Last year Thomas had succumbed to complications of AIDS, but his family had announced that his death was due to cancer. The truth of the matter was that Thomas had acquired cancer subsequent to AIDS. He had developed a brain tumor, along with Kaposi's sarcoma, and since he had refused treatment, his fight for survival was shortened. Thomas became a stranger to his family as his disease progressed. He no longer recognized Denise, a nd her parents were devastated when he became so sick that he was placed in hospice care. The staff was nice, but nothing could prepare them for what he would endure. He was covered in sores that wouldn't heal. His organs became compromised as the disease ravaged his body. He had lost all his mental faculties and stared into space at no one in particular. The simple task of breathing even became a struggle. Thomas's weight dropped dramatically from a healthy two hundred ten pounds to match his height of six two, to a mere ninety-six pounds at the time of his death. Denise knew that even though these were her friends, they could never understand her brother's plight. Throughout history military men had traveled the world, picking up sexually transmitted diseases along the way. Most of these STDs were treated then soon forgotten about. Denise had heard stories of men being exposed to gonorrhea, herpes, and syphilis during overseas tours and bringing them back to their wives and girlfriends. Thomas had come home after being discharged from the military, became a recluse, and quietly made his exit, leaving behind neither a wife nor child.

Standing to stretch her legs, Denise walked to the open window and away from the searing topic as the women gave another round of "Amen to that!" She'd hoped they would move the conversation along to a lighter subject. She was grateful when Carmen asked her if she wasn't feeling well.

"Just nervous. I don't have a lot of time to plan this wedding," she said with a weak smile.

"That's what we're here for!" Carmen said, standing to join her friend.

"Of course! Let's get busy on your plans," Jocelyn added.

The women abandoned the subject at hand and turned their attention to Denise and her upcoming bridal shower. The three friends had planned to host it. Denise's face lit up as the women crowded around her and gave her their undivided attention.

Jocelyn got excited about male strippers and the thought of them forcing their oversize bodies into tiny Speedos. "Girl, I know a stripper who'll make you forget your name!" she said.

"Strippers?" Denise nervously ran her fingers through her hair.

"No one said anything about strippers!" Carmen looked at Jocelyn in disbelief.

Jocelyn sounded disappointed. "What's a bachelorette party without strippers?" "It's going to be a clean party!" Cheryl interjected.

"Well, have it your way!" Jocelyn sat down on the couch, draped an arm across her waist, and placed a hand under her chin.

"No need to pout, you big baby. It's what Denise wants for her bachelorette party," Cheryl said.

"She wants to get married and stay married," Carmen added. "You know what goes on at those parties that Jocelyn attends."

Jocelyn crossed her legs, saying nothing. The look on her face told anyone looking that she was unhappy with the women's decision not to invite the scantily clad men to dance at the party.

"Don't worry, Denise. We're going to have a nice, respectable party for you." Cheryl looked at Jocelyn for affirmation. Jocelyn sucked her teeth, shifted her weight, and tilted her head toward the window.

With Cheryl in the driver's seat, the party was sure to be tame.

26

A wave of nausea swept over Tonya as she sat at her desk, trying to complete her quarterly budget report. She wanted to have it ready before her supervisor came around asking for it. Last month her balance sheet was off by more than $1,500. She didn't need to get a write-up on top of everything else that was going on in her life. Grabbing her wastebasket, she relieved herself of her lunch. The metallic taste of the medication she'd taken that morning lingered on her tongue. If her medication was making her sick, she could just imagine what it was doing to her baby. She was unable to keep anything in her stomach without it coming back to revisit her within minutes. She opened the water bottle she kept at her desk, poured a cap full into a napkin, and placed the wet compress to her forehead. The room was spinning on its own axis, and she wanted off this ride. Maybe she should take the rest of the day off; she wouldn't be able to get much work done in this condition, especially with the constant ringing of the phone. As she closed her eyes and rubbed her temples, the ticking of the clock seemed to be magnified. She gritted her teeth as each swing of the hand hit its mark. Who knew a clock could be so loud? Tonya grabbed her purse from her desk drawer; she needed to go home and lie down.

As she stood to leave, she felt dizzy and lightheaded, so she eased back down into her chair. She had forgotten about her doctor's warning about changing position too fast. She slowly stood, bracing the desk while allowing her body to adapt to the change from a sitting position to a standing one. She'd hate to hit the floor again. The last time she had fallen, she'd ended up with a nice shiner right above her right eye. It looked as if she had grown a horn.

Her office phone lit up and shrilled, indicating a transferred call was waiting for her. Looking at the phone in disgust, she let it roll over to her voice mail.

She picked up the second line and informed her supervisor of her urgent need to take the rest of the day off.

As Tonya passed Mary's desk, she heard her whisper into the receiver. Obviously she was gossiping about someone. Spotting Tonya with her purse on her shoulder, she stopped long enough to inquire about Tonya's plans.

"Leaving early?"

"Yeah, I'm not feeling well."

"Take it easy! Hope you feel better!" she replied, before putting the phone back to her ear.

Tonya flipped the "out" marker by her name on the board, letting the staff know she'd be gone for the rest of the day. She shook her head as she continued to the elevator; she couldn't understand how Mary ever got any work done, considering how much time she spent on the phone discussing other people's business.

The walk to the car was a task in itself; Tonya felt every pebble under her feet. She felt so off balance that even the light breeze threatened her equilibrium. Sitting in the car, she decided to wait until she was able to see straight enough to drive. She was experiencing double vision, which usually was accompanied by ringing in her ears. She'd never been diagnosed with Meniere's disease or any inner-ear problems, but her symptoms mirrored those of Ms. Augustine, her father's neighbor. Ms. Augustine had to give up driving because her dizziness and ringing in her ears had gotten so bad that she compared them to seizures.

Slowing backing out of her parking space, Tonya prayed for a safe drive home.

The drive, however, was much like her walk to the car—sensory overload. She felt every dip, bump, and curve. Tonya was grateful to arrive at Carmen's house safely and in one piece. She knew she needed to get some rest; perhaps she was doing too much. Feeling physically spent, she sprawled across the bed. She regretted not being able to keep her dinner date with Sister Peggy, but her body was an unwilling participant. She'd have to call her now, because Sister Peggy was always on time whenever she had made plans.

"Sister Peggy, I'm sorry to have to call you at such short notice, but I won't be able to keep our dinner date this evening." Tonya's voice was weak and choppy.

"Honey, you don't sound too good. Are you all right?"

Tonya heard the concern in Sister Peggy's voice and didn't want to worry her. "Just too much activity. I'll be fine after I get some rest. I'll see you tomorrow at choir rehearsal." Tonya felt guilty for having to cancel, but she knew she'd be poor company and didn't want Sister Peggy to endure her bouts of sickness.

—⚏—

The next evening Tonya got dressed to attend choir rehearsal. Despite her will to show up, she didn't feel any better. She had asked Carmen to drive, since she still was increasingly short of breath. Tonya dreaded having to go to the bathroom so frequently, but her growing baby was pressing on her bladder so much that she was going to the bathroom every twenty-five minutes. After wobbling into the bathroom stall and locking the door, she plopped down on the seat to rest. The walk from the car to the church had taken a lot out of her. The warm urine burned on its way down; Tonya placed her hand over her mouth to muffle her scream as the feeling of hot acid touched her labia. Each trip to the bathroom was torture.

Tonya heard heavy footsteps enter the bathroom. She peered through the slit between the door and the stall and saw two teenage girls standing before the mirror, fixing their hair and makeup. Tonya recognized them as Felicia, Sister Peggy's daughter, and Melody, a new church member.

"Girl, did you hear about Patrick—oh, I mean, Patricia?" Felicia asked with a giggle.

"What's he up to now?" Melody asked, while applying a new coat of lipstick.

"Word on the street is that he's got the package." Tonya knew Felicia was referring to the kids called AIDS.

"What! Who told you that?"

"I overheard my mom talking to Sister White about him last week."

"Well, he did look kind of sick the last time he came to church. I'll make sure I don't sit anywhere near him on Sunday."

"Melody, you can't get it from sitting next to people. You have to have sex with them!"

"Well, I'm still not getting near him."

"Are you afraid he'll make you gay?" Felicia asked sarcastically.

"Who knows? He might want to give me a holy kiss or something!"

The girls giggled and made kissing sounds at each other.

"You know, he got kicked out of the choir when he came to church dressed as Patricia," Felicia said.

"Yeah, I heard Sister White was so embarrassed that she was quiet all during Sunday service—not a single 'Amen' from her."

"I heard Brother Melvin had the bug before he became a member, and now he's dating Sister Brenda. Do you think he'll give her AIDS if they get married?"

"Not if they only hold hands," Melody said.

"You're such a smart mouth! But on the real, don't you think that's dangerous, even for people in the church?"

"Yeah, but do you think it's true?"

"It's believable. Who knows where he was before he joined to the church," Felicia said.

"My mom says God is omnipotent and can heal you of anything."

"You ever heard of people being healed of AIDS?"

"No," Melody said. "But I'm sure it's been done."

"I ain't never heard of nobody being healed of AIDS."

"Maybe somewhere in Africa or somewhere, or maybe those people on TV who are always praying for people, and they fall on the floor."

"Just make sure that it's not your testimony!" Felicia said.

The girls laughed as they finished applying their makeup and left the bathroom.

Tonya sat still in the stall, shocked at what she'd heard. She felt guilty for eavesdropping, but she couldn't just come out of the stall and announce to the girls that she'd overheard them. Her mind began to wander. *Would they say those horrible things about me if they found out?* She could never tell a single soul outside of the family about her status, not even Sister Peggy.

Elder Lacey always had taught her to love others despite their differences, but people could be so cruel when it came to things of this magnitude. Fear causes people to hate others, and lack of understanding causes them to ostracize those who are infected. Tonya knew you can't get HIV from talking to people, sitting next to them, or even hugging them, but fear of the unknown is the most powerful catalyst for hate.

She remembered the day when Patrick had announced to everyone that he was gay and transgender and that he would no longer live a lie. It was no secret to anyone who knew Patrick that he was transgender; his appearance alone was a walking billboard. He always wore brightly colored clothing and was more feminine than most women. He was meticulous about having his clothes pressed and starched and his shoes spotless. So no one was surprised when he made his announcement. The boy could put a woman to shame when it came to hair and fashion.

When boys his age wore baggy pants and oversize shirts, Patrick wore slim-fitting jeans and slacks. His shirts were always pastel colors that hugged his slim body. He also was fond of wearing boots. *The closest thing to high heels*, Tonya thought. He spoke with perfect grammar, instead of the slang kids his age used. He was just a different kind of boy. Over the years he had grown on Tonya, and she accepted him for himself.

The day he had announced that he wanted to be called "Patricia," he wore eyeliner and mascara to bring out his eyes. Looking like Stoney Jackson in the 1980s crime show *The Insiders*, Patrick chose to make his announcement in the middle of choir rehearsal. Sister White was beside herself with embarrassment. This turned choir rehearsal out! There was no singing that day. Poor Daryl had to dismiss rehearsal and ask the choir to regroup the following week.

Tonya slowly made her way to the choir stand. The walk from the ladies' room to the sanctuary had been tiring. Sitting next to Carmen while the choir waited for Daryl to arrive, she whispered, "We need to leave early, and if he's not here in the next twenty minutes, let's jet." Daryl was never late and never would cancel rehearsal without calling the choir members. Tonya knew some-thing must be very serious to keep him from being at rehearsal. After the group had waited for thirty minutes, Sister Peggy finally was able to contact Daryl on his cell phone and was told that D.J. was in the emergency room. He had suf-fered a broken arm after falling off his bicycle. Deacon Frazier accompanied Sister Peggy to give the choir members the news. He led the group in prayer for little D.J.'s recovery. After the longwinded prayer, with Deacon Frazier all but praying for Lazarus's resurrection, the choir members left collectively.

Tonya spotted Melody and Felicia walking toward Felicia's car. Giggling and talking fast, the girls jumped into the car and sped off. Tonya imagined them talking about her after they found out she was ill and all the nasty things they'd say about her and the evil looks they'd probably give her. Tears trickled down her cheeks as she sat next to Carmen on the drive home. The incident in the bathroom reminded her of how ignorant people could be about the disease and how meanly they treated others once they'd gotten wind of their status. The treatment by others that often follows disclosure is one reason those infected remained quiet. Tonya wondered just how much her sister knew about the disease and whether she was afraid of her as well.

"Carmen," she said, "do you think could give you HIV by living with you?"

"What do you mean? Where's this coming from?"

"I overheard some girls talking in the bathroom about catching AIDS from sitting next to a person."

Carmen rolled her eyes. "That's crazy! I love you very much and would never treat you in such a manner. When you told me you were sick, I did my homework so I wouldn't be in the dark. So no, I'm not one of those people who thinks that."

"Thanks. It just scares me when people look at people like me like they can get HIV from just being near us."

"You don't need to worry about that from me. If I felt you were a danger to me, I'd tell you."

"What about the night I went to the hospital? I was bleeding and leaking amniotic fluid. Weren't you alarmed that you might come into contact with my bodily fluids?"

"Tonya, I took precautions. I wore gloves and stripped your bed. I also washed your bedding in bleach. I wasn't afraid of catching it as long as I was careful when I handled anything that might have your fluids on it."

Tonya smiled. "When did you get so smart?"

"I had to know how to live with you and not be afraid of you. There's a wealth of knowledge on the Internet. The World Health Organization and the Centers for Disease Control provide a great deal of information."

Tonya squeezed Carmen's hand. "I must say I'm impressed!"

"Before I read about HIV, I didn't have a clue how people actually contracted it. I was as misguided as most people when it came to the matter. I used to believe you could get it by touching, hugging, or kissing someone with HIV. I was as scared of it as most people. Fear comes from lack of knowledge, so in order to cage that fear, I had to educate myself. HIV is contracted through the transfer of blood and blood products. It's spread by unprotected sex that involves semen and vaginal fluids, childbirth by an infected mother, the use of contaminated needles, deep kissing, and breast-feeding. Oh, and get this—breast-feeding isn't just for babies anymore, if you get my drift. There are a lot of grown men who still breast-feed."

Tonya blushed at what Carmen was insinuating. Even though she was married, she didn't feel comfortable talking about things that went on between a man and a woman, especially with her little sister.

"Now I know more about HIV than I did before," Carmen continued, "and I feel comfortable living with you."

"You really did do your homework."

"I was afraid I'd offend you, but safety first, right?"

"Safety first!" Tonya smiled and put her arm around her sister's shoulders. She felt much better knowing she wasn't afraid of her. "Thank you, Carmen."

"What's with the gratitude?"

"I'm grateful for having a great sister and a wonderful friend. You've put a smile on my face and joy in my heart. It's so hard to carry this burden, but God placed you in my life for a reason."

"Tonya, I'm your sister. I've always been in your life, and I always will be."

"I know, but not all sisters get along. You're a fantastic sister, and I believe God placed you in my life for times like these."

"I believe you're right, because I've seen some of those episodes of *The Jerry Springer Show* with families pulling each other's hair out."

Tonya burst out laughing, again glad for having such a warm, loving sister in Carmen.

27

Keith's nerves were rattled as he waited to be called into Dr. Gipson's office. He couldn't stop his hands from wringing water. He had rubbed his sweat-soaked hands on his pant legs until he was starting to stretch the fabric. The reason for his doctor's visit infuriated him the more he thought about it. *How could people like Shayla be allowed to walk around free?* he wondered. *Don't they lock up people with AIDS who knowingly spread it to other people? They should be given the death penalty.* He'd been waiting only twenty minutes, but it seemed like an hour had passed since he'd arrived. He was becoming unglued as he sat and waited. "Hurry up, Doc," he mumbled, biting his bottom lip.

Keith walked up to the reception window, where a different woman was working than the usual receptionist. She was a little older but not bad looking.

"Excuse me," he said. "Can you tell me how much longer I have to wait to be seen?"

"Your name, sir?"

"Keith Paris."

Looking at the sign-in sheet, she replied, "Not long. You should be next."

"What's 'not long'?"

"Less than ten minutes. The nurse will come out and get you shortly."

"Thanks."

Keith took note as to how courteous this new receptionist was in comparison to the biddy he'd encountered during his last visit. She would have closed the window on him, leaving him standing there looking dumb. He hated coming to the doctor's office when she was there, because of her rather unpleasant demeanor. Keith wanted to tell her to find another job if she didn't like this one, because she was making his life miserable. Maybe she'd gotten a clue and bounced on her own.

The ten minutes seemed to be drawn out as he waited for the nurse to call his name. A young man came in with hacking cough. He didn't seem to know how to cover his mouth as he opened his mouth and coughed up whatever was lodged in his chest. Keith quickly moved to a different seat to avoid the spittle. He eyeballed a young man not far from him who was wearing a pink button-down shirt and tight jeans. His fingernails were manicured, and his hair was in neat dreadlocks. The guy looked at Keith, crossed his legs, and fluttered his lashes.

"Sorry, dude. I don't swing that way!" Keith said with disdain in his voice.

Clearly feeling dejected, the young man pushed his lips up in a pout and tossed his head, which caused his hair to swing in his face. He rolled his eyes as he shifted in his chair, turning away from Keith.

The nurse came from the behind the door that led to the exam rooms and called him in to see the doctor. Keith was glad to leave the waiting area, the man with the hacking cough, and the flirtatious diva.

Dr. Gipson took a while before he came into the exam room to see Keith. When he finally arrived, Keith was sitting on the end of the exam table, rocking back and forth, trying to control his nerves.

After knocking on the door, Dr. Gipson entered the room with Keith's medical chart in hand. "Mr. Paris, how are you doing today?"

How do you think I'm doing? I'm about to lose my mind! he thought.

"Nervous, a little anxious," Keith told Dr. Gipson.

"Well, I did get your test result, so let's talk about what they mean."

As Keith walked out of the doctor's office, the young man who had been eyeing him earlier was no longer sitting there, which was a relief, because he didn't want to have to kick his butt for leering at him. He was in no mood for that nonsense.

As he pulled out of the parking lot, he felt the need for a strong drink. He headed toward Rob's Place, hoping he wouldn't run into anyone he knew; he especially wasn't feeling up for Darlene's madness today. He was shocked when Dr. Gipson had given him his diagnosis. Dr. Gipson had ordered multiple tests that revealed that Keith not only had HIV but also was positive for hepatitis B, which wasn't something he had expected. What did this all mean?

Dr. Gipson also had spoken to him about medication, more lab tests, and some CD4 levels, which all flew over Keith's head. How could he think about this when the doctor had just told him he had HIV? What person in his right mind wants to talk about living when he's just been given a death sentence? In addition to hepatitis C, he also had contracted herpes. Keith wondered what the hell was going on with his body. How could he have been carrying all these diseases without knowing it?

As he walked into the bar, he suddenly felt the urge to turn around and walk back out. He spotted Darlene sitting the corner with her bony arms draped around some unsuspecting older brother. She was wearing the same outfit she'd had on the last time Keith was there.

He held his tongue as he took a seat at the bar and ordered his drink. He wanted to scold Denise about not being with her children, but he knew his words would fall on deaf ears. The brother looked as if he'd had one too many shots and could hardly stand on his own two feet. T-Bone and Keith watched the pair as Darlene fished her crooked fingers into the man's jacket pocket, pulled out a wad of cash, and slipped it into her bra.

Keith bounced off the barstool. "Hey, fellow. Wake up! You're being robbed."

The man reached into his pocket and realized his cash was missing. He grabbed a beer bottle from the table, smashed it in two, and held the sharp glass to Darlene's throat as he grabbed her by the back of her head. "Heifer, you give me my money back or meet yo' maker up in here!"

Darlene quickly pulled the money from its hiding place, threw it on the table, and ran for the door. By the way she jumped up, Keith knew she was up to no good. The man counted the money tossed in front of him. Unsatisfied with what Darlene had produced, he stuffed the money into his pocket and ran out the door after her, demanding the rest of his cash.

"Looks like Darlene done met her match!" T-Bone said.

"I couldn't let her gyp that old dude like that!"

"If she had any sense, she would have asked him for some money. That's Carl Wright. He's seen more time on the inside than he's ever seen on the outside. Folks say he was born in prison. When he was ten, he shot his old man for hitting his mom."

"How long has he been out?" Keith asked.

"About three weeks. He just did a fifteen-year stretch for hacking up his old woman. I don't believe he'd think twice about putting a hurting on Darlene. She tries to gyp at least ten fellows a week. Sometimes they catch her; sometimes they don't. That woman's got more lives than a cat!"

Darlene had been in the hospital two years ago, after a woman had shot her for fooling around with her husband. Darlene had confronted the man's wife at her home during a drunken spell and didn't have the sense to leave when the woman threatened her with a pistol. She stretched out her arms like a brave soldier and told the woman to shoot her if she thought she was so bad. Before she could repeat her request, the woman shot her in the chest. Darlene lived only because no vital organs had been hit. A month after the incident, she was back with the same man. Some people never learn.

Forgetting his reason for coming to Rob's Place, Keith skipped the drink and headed home. He'd seen enough crazy for the day.

As he walked into the house, he felt his cell phone vibrate on his hip.

"Hey, man. Where you been?" Jerry asked him.

"Busy. What's up?"

"Take a ride with me!"

"Where to?"

"Nowhere. Let's just ride!"

If anyone else had asked him to take a ride with no destination in mind, Keith would have declined, but he trusted Jerry.

When Jerry picked him up, he was quiet, so Keith figured something was up. "Where's Brian?" he asked. Jerry and Brian always rode together, because none of them wanted to be left out on anything.

"We'll meet him later. I wanted to talk to you before we meet up with him."

"Sure. What's up?" Keith knew something was coming.

"I bumped into Jimmy, the mechanic, and he told me Shayla died. Rumor has it she had AIDS. Did you know?"

Feeling like a scorned child, Keith dropped his head. "I found out a few weeks ago."

"What about you? I mean, you were sleeping with her. Did you use protection?"

Tears flowed freely from Keith's eyes as he tried to explain the torment he'd endured since he'd found out about Shayla. He became incoherent as he relayed to Jerry what the doctor had shared with him about his diagnosis.

"So you gave the virus to Tonya, huh?"

"Yeah. I didn't know…I was never sick. Now the doctor tells me I've got it. Out of nowhere he tells me I've got it!"

"Why didn't you use protection? We told you the type of woman she was from the start."

"I know, but you saw her. She didn't look sick."

"When are people going to learn that no one walks around with an HIV sign stuck to their chest? Man, it's up to us to protect ourselves."

As the men pulled up to pick up Brian, a fresh stream of tears flowed from Keith's eyes. He knew Brian would be even more critical than Jerry, but he deserved to hear every word.

Keith broke the news to Brian, who sat back and let the unsettling information sink in. Brian wasn't one to be soft on him when it came to stupidity. Keith waited for his reaction. The men decided to go to a local sports bar to watch the New York Mets in action and discuss the issue at hand. Sipping on his second Long Island iced tea, Jerry broached the subject. Watching him, Keith laughed to himself. *For a dude, he drinks like a woman.* Jerry didn't drink alcoholic beverages, but he was in for a shock if he thought he could handle drinking two rounds of Long Island iced tea back to back.

"Keith, have you told Tonya yet?" Jerry asked.

"Not yet, but I think she knows. How could she not know?"

Brian piped in for the first time since Keith told him the news. "You owe her an apology."

"Why would a person who knows they're infected not tell anyone else? She could have told me to cover up. Man, why don't they lock up people like that?"

"Look," Brian said, "this is a free country. Shayla didn't stick you with a needle and infect you. You made a conscious decision to sleep with her, and I might add."

"All I'm saying is that if I had TB and refused treatment and refused to wear a mask out in public, I'd be locked up!"

"That's different. TB is spread through breathing on people or coming into contact with their mucus, but HIV is a sexually transmitted disease. No one forced you to sleep with Shayla."

"Last I recall, we warned you about her, but nooo, she was your boo!" Jerry said, as he finished his drink.

"I know. I was blinded."

"Did you consider using a condom so she wouldn't get pregnant?" Brian asked.

Keith took a sip of his Rémy. "She said she was on the pill."

Brian and Jerry hooted simultaneously.

"Man, that's for the birds! No one has lived this long and not heard of that game. Are you that naive? Women learn that trick at age sixteen!" Jerry said, as he motioned for the waitress to bring him another drink.

"Hey, easy on the drinks, man." Brian warned.

"Don't worry about him. I'll drive back. Besides, I left my car at his place," Keith said, shaking his head at Jerry.

Halfway through his third Long Island, Jerry became a man of few words. Keith knew he'd feel it in the morning.

"Look who's calling someone naive. The dude thought he was drinking plain iced tea," Keith said. He and Brian both laughed as Jerry sat spaced out.

"He may be toasted, but what he said makes sense, so don't count him out just yet. Your old man should have told you to always protect yourself. I didn't have a dad growing up, but my mom threatened me so much about bringing her a baby that I made sure I didn't. I was too scared she'd beat the brakes from under me, like she always said she would."

"Well, my pops didn't talk about that kind of stuff with me, but it's not like I didn't know. I just slipped up with Shayla."

"Man, Shayla was a regular Heather Mac Swoon!"

"What's that?" Keith asked, not hip to the terminology.

"A girl who swoons over any macdaddy she thinks has money."

Laughing at Brian's description of Shayla, Keith couldn't deny that he had summed her up perfectly. "Dang! That's exactly what she was, because she bled my checking account dry!"

"Let me be the first to say, 'I told you so!' " Jerry said, slurring his words as he lifted his glass as if giving a toast.

28

Annoyed by the constant ringing of the phone, Jerry finally snatched the receiver from its cradle. "Yeah?" The clock on his nightstand read 3:15 a.m.

"Jerry…hey, man, I couldn't sleep."

"Well, I could. What's up?"

"K.J."

"What about him?"

"Can you believe it, man?" Brian said. "He's got HIV."

"Yeah, that's what he said."

"Do you think he gave it to Tonya instead of what he told us?"

"Look, man, I'm still out of it. Let me get back to you when I'm sober."

"Oh, OK." *Click.*

Brian looked at the phone after hearing the dial tone. *Dude, learn to say good-bye!*

Jerry called Brian back after taking a couple of aspirin for his hangover and getting some sleep. The two decided to take in a game of pool at a bar and grill that afternoon.

"What do you think about all this?" Jerry asked.

"I don't know, but I can say the man is foul for what he did to his wife," Brian said, as he banked the six ball into the left corner pocket.

"Well, I agree, but I just wish he'd listened to us. We told him about that girl. She was nothing but trouble, and he—"

"Jerry, you can't save everybody. He's a grown man who knew what he was doing." Brian shook his head. "You can't save 'em all."

The two men played another game of pool before calling it quits.

Sitting down at the bar, Brian grabbed a beer. Jerry ordered a ginger ale.

"What! No Long Island?" Brian teased.

"Naw, man. I won't do that again. I'll stick to what I know."

"So do you think it's catchy?"

Jerry knew what Brian was referring to. "Of course, but who's trying to get close enough to catch it? Our b-ball days are over! I'm not roughhousing with anybody who's that lethal!"

Brian raised his glass. "I hear that!"

The men sat in silence as they attempted to digest the new information. It was a hard pill to swallow as they tried to come to terms with how their friendship with Keith might change.

Brian's cell phone vibrated. Looking at his caller ID, he elected to ignore the call. Two minutes later, Jerry received the same call and followed suit. Neither was ready to face Keith.

"What do we say to him? 'Sorry, man. Now step back'?" Brian mumbled.

"I'm not afraid of him, but I don't know enough about that crap to be around him. What if he gets a nosebleed or wants to give us a high-five or something?"

"Exactly," Brian interjected.

"I feel guilty for abandoning him at a time like this, but it's hard to deal with this."

"You're preaching to the choir, man. I'm walking right beside you."

29

Keith dialed six digits then quickly hung up the phone. He couldn't bring himself to make the call. *What could I possibly say to her to make her forgive me?* He didn't know whether he would be as forgiving if the shoe were on the other foot. Willing himself to complete the task at hand, he dialed Tonya's cell number. When she didn't answer, Keith wondered whether she was refusing his calls or was actually busy. His call was forwarded to her voice mail, which instructed him to leave a name, number, and a brief message. Not wanting to leave a detailed message, he just asked her to call him. *I'd hate to make a confession over the phone. Besides, who wants to hear something so personal on their voice mail?* Keith thought, as he hung up the phone. Not expecting Tonya to call back, he decided to try to reach her another day; maybe she just didn't want to be bothered. He could understand if he was the last person she wanted to talk to.

Checking her cell-phone messages after she ended her prayer session with Sister Peggy, Tonya noticed she had six missed calls. As she listened to her voice mails, she froze when she heard Keith's voice. *What would possess him to call me after all this time?* she thought. It had been four and a half months since she and Keith had separated. She had been praying that God would mend her marriage before she gave birth to their son. Maybe this was a sign from God, but what exactly was he telling her?

"What did he want?" Carmen asked, after Tonya relayed Keith's message later that day.

"I don't know. I didn't call back to ask him."

"He needs to get a life! He's done enough damage already."

"Maybe I should call him. It could be important."

Carmen rolled her eyes. "The only thing he needs to tell you is that he's going to jump off the Empire State Building without a parachute."

"Carmen, that was very ugly!"

"And what he did to you wasn't?"

"What if his call is a sign from God?"

"A sign?"

"Well, I have been praying for him—for us."

"Are you kidding me? That man wrecked your life. He literally beat you down and didn't care if he killed you and your unborn child, and you've been praying for him?"

"We've all done things we aren't proud of, things we'd never do in our right mind."

"So now you're saying he's mentally ill?" Carmen asked.

"No, but I am saying this situation would be devastating to anyone's psyche."

"There you go again, making excuses for him."

Tonya sighed deeply. Carmen could never understand the love she had for her Keith.

She decided to call Keith when she could talk. She needed to be far away from Carmen and her barrage of questions and advice.

When Tonya called Keith that evening, he had no idea how to start the conversation. He didn't want to put his heart on the line only to have it destroyed. He was in a vulnerable state, and the last thing he wanted to deal with was rejection. He began by telling Tonya about a letter that had arrived at the house from her college roommate. The two women rarely spoke over the phone but had kept in contact by sending letters, cards, and photos over the years. After telling her about the letter, which was trivial, he stumbled over his explanation for calling. *I've got to tell her,* he kept telling himself.

After he'd found the courage to break the news to Tonya that he was infected with HIV, he feared she would hate him even more then shut him out of her life forever. At this time in his life, he didn't need any more people shutting him out like he was a bad omen. Jerry and Brian hadn't exactly shut him out, but they hadn't called or come around after the initial shock. Their last meeting at the sports bar a week or so ago was the last he'd seen of his friends. Whenever he'd called since then, they were always too busy to hang out, or they didn't answer his calls. Keith had left several messages on his friends' cell phones, but neither of them had returned his calls. Keith finally got it. He couldn't lose Tonya too, so he swallowed his pride and begged his wife to come back home.

"Life just isn't the same without you. My days are filled with thoughts of you, wondering what you are doing, how the pregnancy is coming along and how you are dealing with being sick. My nights are lonely; I roll over in bed and find you not lying next to me. It's all just a reminder of the damage I've caused to our marriage. I promise that if you take me back I will be a better husband and father. I will fix this mess that I've made if you will just forgive me and come back home. I will even spend more time in church, giving God what's left of my life. I know that I complained about how much time you spent at church, but look at what being out of church and running away from God did for me. I have destroyed my marriage and jeopardized my life."

Tonya could hear the sorrow in his voice and knew that he was sincere; she too wanted to work on her marriage. She didn't realize that she'd been crying until tears dropped into her lap as she held the phone in her trembling hands. Before she accepted his apology she had to know just one more.

"It may not seem like much to you, but I need to know who is she and how did we go so wrong?"

Keith took his time before answering her question. "She's no one."

"Well, that no one nearly caused us our marriage."

"I've ended it. I have put that behind me and want my family back." His voice cracked as he attempted to convince Tonya of his sincerity. This was all she needed. She felt relieved that things were being rectified and her life was being put back together.

Standing in front of the church in her wedding gown, Tonya looked at Keith, who seemed very anxious—well, more like a nervous wreck. Carmen stood to her left. She wore a beautiful

smile that was warm and reassuring, sending a silent message that everything would be fine. The church was filled to capacity. The organ played a soft love song as the choir hummed along. The church was elegantly decorated with flowers and candles. At the end of each row was a small bouquet of white flowers, tied to the pew by yards of translucent silk. The guests smiled at her as she took in each face. The minister for ceremony, Pastor Mullin, stood before the young couple in his black-and-gold clergy robe, looking debonair as he performed the ceremony.

"Do you, Tonya, take this man to be your lawfully wedded husband, to live together in the covenant of matrimony? Will you love him comfort him, honor him, and keep him, in sickness and in health, and forsaking all others, be faithful to him as long as you both shall live?"

As she opened her mouth to respond, she saw Keith lying in a hospital bed with tubes in his arms and a breathing apparatus in his mouth. No longer were the two standing before their family and friends. She heard the machines beeping and saw the monitor with the lines indicating that his heart was beating. Then the machine made an eerie sound as Keith flat lined.

Tonya jumped out of the frightening nightmare. She tried to decipher the dream, but everything seemed so confusing and fussy. Could it mean that she had made him sick? She tried to think of any possible way she could have infected Keith, and then she remembered that one incident in college. In sheer turmoil, Tonya replayed the dreadful night of her sophomore year.

Tonya and her roommate Monica had planned for weeks to go to the homecoming game. The temperature had dropped to the 30s, so Tonya worn her knee length boots, her team spirit sweatshirt, and a new pair of Calvin Klein's and bomber jacket. The stands were packed with spectators, energy soaring as the fans cheered for their team to score the next touchdown. As the time clock wind down, people began to flood the parking lot, celebrating long after the game had ended. Tonya and Monica returned to their dorm room to rest for the after party. Both girl were restless and on cloud nine and not ready to call it a day. They had gotten invitations from every fraternity on campus. Homecoming weekend was party weekend. She was going to enjoy herself. *You only live once.* She told herself as she prepared to enjoy this night.

The girls decided to meet up with a few of the girls from the dorm to see which party was the hottest. Sharon, a known party-goer, suggested that they swing over to the Kappa house. Deborah, a junior majoring in spending daddy's money, had an even better idea. "Let hit em all! Deborah had been in college for four years already and still couldn't decide what she wanted to do with her life. She had started out with a major in Education, but changed to Business, later changed to Psychology, now majoring in Liberal Arts. The girls looked up to Deborah since she was the oldest of the group, not that she was wiser.

Toward the end of the night, Tonya had drank so many cup of spiked punch, sample from several kegs of beer and indirectly inhaled so much marijuana that her head was spinning. She had tagged along with the girls, but she couldn't remember where she was and how she'd gotten separated from the group. What she did remember was someone tugging on her jeans. Her mind was so fizzled that she thought she was being helped to the bathroom by one of her friends. She had drunk so much that it was going right through her. Tonya tried to rise, but her body was so heavy. She was lying in a bed, but it wasn't hers. She tried again to get up, but something or someone was holding her down. She was startled when she realized that she was not alone. She fought to stop someone from pulling her underwear down, but she was no match against this person.

"Hold her man, she's waking up" she heard someone whisper.

"Hurry up, I'm next" a second voice responded.

Tonya opened her eyes to see not two, but five or six guys standing over her waiting for their turn with her. She tried to scream, but a large hand clamped over her mouth to silence her. As the first guy entered her with force, Tonya began to cry as she struggled to free herself. This was not how she has planned to lose her virginity. One after the other the boys took turns, disregarding her pleas as they cheered each other on. She tried to focus on their faces, but her vision was blurred. She saw tattoos on their biceps and bare chest of fraternity insignias, black panthers, tigers and snakes, but she couldn't place the tattoos with the faces. She had no idea where she was or who had done this awful thing to her, because after the guys were finish using her, they threw her in the back of a small jalopy, drove her a mile from campus and dropped her off. She had to walk back to campus. She was cold, soiled with urine and had vomited on her new boots. Her night couldn't get any worse. When she finally reached her dorm room, Monica was nowhere to be found. Maybe she was still out having a ball, but Tonya had been through hell. She never told a soul about that night, not even her roommate.

How could I have been so stupid? she thought. *I should have known better.* She blamed herself for possibly having exposed herself to HIV. She began to consider the validity of Keith's previous accusation of her giving him the virus. *Maybe he was right. Maybe I'm being punished for keeping this secret. It's my fault!*

—⁂—

"Are you crazy? How could you even consider going back?" Carmen screamed at Tonya when she told her she was moving back home. The two women sat across from each other eating a meal prepared by Tonya. She had attempted to replicate Sister's White's homemade Chicken and Dumpling recipe. Carmen cooked the southern style buttermilk corn bread in which she took pride.

"At least we can be together for our child."

"Tonya, you can't possibly be serious about this." Carmen pushed her plate away, she had suddenly lost her appetite.

"Maybe I wouldn't be in this situation if I'd spent more time with my husband than at church."

"This has nothing to do with your church duties or your duties as a wife," Carmen said. "Keith made a sound decision to cheat on you! You can't take the blame—it doesn't make the situation any easier to place the blame on yourself."

The two women went back and forth on the subject, with Carmen failing to convince her sister to stay. "I am not happy about you going back to him, but it's your decision. Please remember that I will always be here for you no matter the time, place or situation. Tonya believed her dream had been a sign from the Lord that she should honor her marriage vows. "Thank you."

The women embraced. Carmen could never stop loving her sister or let her leave without feeling that she could ever come back the next time Keith screwed up.

"No matter how far you go, know that you can always count on me and should you ever need to come back this way remember I've given you the key."

30

Patrick showed up in rare form on Sunday morning. He marched into the service wearing a flaming-peach suit, a loud peach-and-green tie, and peach shoes to match. He had taken out his braids and was now wearing his hair in thick curls. He wore three layers of makeup, which covered his already light complexion, and his eyes were hidden under a heavy cake of mascara and eyeliner.

Although he wore a great deal of makeup, it couldn't hide the sores on his face, which resembled those of chicken pox. He had a dry, hacking cough that was very annoying throughout the service and elicited frowns from the ushers and those sitting close to him. From her seat in the choir stand, Tonya noticed that the woman who sat next to him had stood up and walked out of the service. Five minutes later the woman returned to the sanctuary but sat on the opposite side of the church, away from Patrick and his coughing fit.

Halfway through Pastor Mullin's sermon, Patrick stood up. "God ain't got nothing to do with this," he exclaimed. "He gonna tear this place down, and everybody in it, because y'all act like only you people in this church are going to heaven!"

Sister White dropped her head in shame at his outburst.

"Young man, you will have to excuse yourself if you cannot conduct yourself in an acceptable manner," Pastor Mullin said.

"This young man has a name, and it's Patricia! I'm a woman, and you will address me as such. Why can't you see this? Look at me—I'm as much a woman as any of y'all. Look at me!"

Sister White rushed to Patrick's side. "Stop this!" she hissed. "You're carrying on something awful!"

"That cancer has gone to his brain," Sister White said, loud enough for everyone to hear.

"Tell it like it is. AIDS—I have AIDS!" Patrick yelled.

"Hush now!" Sister White whispered.

"People like me aren't accepted in this church. We're not accepted anywhere. Where can we go?"

"Son," Pastor Mullin said, "you're always welcome here, but you must conduct yourself in a respectable manner. We don't turn away souls at New Covenant Full Gospel. We embrace you as much as the next person."

"Humph!" Patrick grabbed his backpack. "Tell it to somebody else!" Coughing uncontrollably, he walked out of the service.

With tears streaming down her face, Sister White ran after her son.

Three weeks later Sister White led her son to the altar. Kneeling down, Patrick wept as he repented for his sins, asking God for redemption. The choir softly sang "I Surrender All" as the altar call was conducted. People began to flood the altar.

That morning seventeen people were baptized, Patrick being one of them. As Patrick went down in the water, Sister Peggy once again felt the need to be "dropped-kicked" by Jesus, and Sister White joined her.

31

Sitting at her desk, Tonya received a call from Sabrina, her friend and co-worker, whose office was down the hall from hers.

"Tonya, let's do lunch," Sabrina said. "I really need to talk to you."

"Sure. Is everything OK?"

"Yeah, but I can't talk here. You pick the spot."

Tonya wondered what was going on with Sabrina. Several months ago she had confided in Tonya that her husband abused her and often hit the children in a fit of rage when he was drunk. Tonya had told Sabrina to leave her husband and had given her the number to a local shelter for battered women. It took Sabrina two months to heed Tonya's advice, after her husband had broken their son's arm and social services threatened to take away the child. Tonya couldn't imagine what was bothering Sabrina now.

As they sat across from each other at lunch, both of them neglected the food on their plates. Sabrina gave Tonya a nervous smile as she took a sip of her soda.

"I didn't want to talk to you at the office, because those walls have ears."

Tonya laughed. "You mean Mary has ears."

"Speaking of Mary, I overheard her talking on the phone yesterday. She was trying to whisper, but everybody knows she's much too loud for that."

"Amen!" Tonya chimed in, raising her glass.

"Well, what I overheard her saying was very disturbing. She was telling someone that a friend of her daughter's recently died of AIDS, and word is that she had an affair with your husband and that you probably contracted it from him."

Tonya couldn't believe what she was hearing. As she listened to the details of Mary's telephone conversation, she felt air escape from her body. The sensation left her feeling winded.

"Tonya, are you all right?"

She sat back as the blood returned to her face.

"I know this is shocking to you, but I didn't want you to be the last person to know what's being said around the office concerning you."

"Thanks," Tonya said weakly.

Sabrina leaned forward as she watched Tonya's world come tumbling down.

How dare Mary spread my business around the office like that! Unable to catch her breath, Tonya began to hyperventilate, and the room spun. *Not again!* she thought, as the lights dimmed before fading out.

As Tonya's eyes finally began to focus, she saw Sabrina looking worried while standing over her chair. She couldn't believe it; she had fainted again.

"Tonya, you just vanished for a minute there. Do you have spells or something?"

"'Or something' is right. I don't do well under stressful situations, but I'm OK now."

"I'm sorry for causing you stress. I only wanted to let you know what's being said around the office so you wouldn't be surprised when you heard it."

"That's thoughtful of you," Tonya said. "I guess I should tell you that I can only speak for me. It's true that I'm sick, but I can't speak for Mary's daughter's friend. It's not something people easily talk about, so I wasn't sure how people at work would react. But this does explain why Mary doesn't come to my office or ask me to join her for lunch anymore.

"I'm sorry to hear about your condition. I am here for you should you want to talk about it. I don't know a whole lot about HIV, but I do know that it is not the end of the world. People live long lives with virus, and even work diligently to help others with the disease." Sabrina reached into her handbag and pulled out a small magazine which featured a smiling man posed on the cover. "This is a POZ magazine, it will give you insight as to what being positive is and how to survive. There are HIV positive people who work to make their lives more positive than the virus could ever do."

Taking the magazine from Sabrina, Tonya flipped through the pages as she skimmed testimonies from people affected by HIV. Feeling as if someone would know that she was reading the magazine for herself, she quickly folded the magazine in half and stuffed it in her purse.

"You know, Mary avoiding you could be a blessing in disguise," Sabrina said.

"Last week I sneezed as I walked toward my office. Less than two seconds later, I heard Mary spraying the office. I guess she's afraid I'm going to sneeze hard enough to give her something."

"Tonya, don't let Mary's nonsense get to you. There are going to be people like her who make other people's lives miserable. Just ignore her."

Tonya sighed. "That's easier said than done."

After Sabrina and Tonya returned to work, Tonya didn't see Mary. She'd left early for a doctor's appointment. *It's a good thing she's not here. I'd probably strangle her*, Tonya thought as she headed toward her office. Needing to talk to her best friend, she picked up the phone and dialed Carmen's number.

Tonya told her sister how hurt she felt by Mary's behavior and treatment toward her. "Carmen"I can't believe Mary could be so insensitive. How could she spread my business around the office like that? I've never been so embarrassed in my life. I am too scared to show my face here."

"Don't sweat it. Just stay home and concentrate on your health."

"Who's going to take care of my bills if I don't work?"

"K.J. works."

"But for how much longer, Carmen? He's sick too."

"You could always try to work from home. A lot of people are doing that these days."

Tonya gave the idea some thought. "I'll look into it. I'm sure the company could still use me."

"Well, you know what Sister Peggy always says."

"Let go and let God do his thang!" the two said in unison.

A week later, Tonya collected her pictures, flowers, and personal papers and placed them in a box. She'd made an agreement with her boss to work from home, which would allow her to continue to receive pay. The company even had given her a laptop to take home with her. She was happy to have the opportunity to continue to earn an income.

Mary spied Tonya with her belongings as she passed her office. She jumped at the chance to be the first to find out the news.

"Did you quit?"

"Mary, I believe in the law of reciprocity. If you do good deeds, good will come back to you, but if you sow discord, malice, and confusion, those things will come back to you. Some people call it karma, but whatever your belief is, it's all the same—what goes around comes around."

Mary's jaw dropped as she tried to gather her thoughts.

"So why don't you go back to your desk and finish tearing down somebody else's reputation?" Tonya said. "Because you definitely don't do any work around here!" Not giving Mary a chance to respond, she turned on her heels and walked away.

As Tonya placed the box and laptop into the trunk of her car, her cell phone rang.

"Girl," Sabrina said, "Mary's telling everyone you just quit."

"That's just like her."

"Well, did you? I thought you were going to work from home." Tonya had shared with Sabrina that she had been approved to work from home. She would be able to maintain her income and concentrate on her health.

"No, Sabrina I didn't quit. I'll be working from home instead of taking maternity leave."

"Well, I guess she doesn't know everything."

"Did she ever?" Tonya asked sarcastically.

"Girl, just take care of your baby, and don't worry about Mary, because people like her have short attention spans. This week it's you. Next week it'll be somebody else. What she needs to pay attention to is that matted wig she wears every day. She walks around here looking like a lost zoo critter!"

"I don't have time for Mary and her insecurities," Tonya said.

"Don't worry about her. I'll handle her on this end. You just get some rest and take care of your baby."

"Thanks, Sabrina. I'll give you a call once I get settled this evening."

After leaving work, Tonya decided to go to the park since it was early in the day, and it was so beautiful out. She spotted a group of young boys playing tee ball. The team of pint-size ball players was a sight to see. After the pitcher threw the ball, the batter hit it past first base. Two boys on the opposing team ran after the ball, each pushing the other in an attempt to be the one to retrieve. The two boys ran screaming, "I got it" as they shoved each other to get the rolling ball. The coach yelled, "Grab the ball! Grab the ball!"

After one of the boys reached the ball, the other tyke tackled him, grabbed it, and ran across the field to first base before throwing it to the pitcher. By this time the hitter had made it safely to home plate. *I'm not sure what sport this is,* Tonya thought as she chuckled, *softball, football, track, or wrestling.*

Watching the little boys play made her feel a lot better. It took her mind off her problems—if only for a moment.

32

Pastor Mullin taught the Wednesday Bible class from the Book of James, chapter one, verse twenty-six—"If any man among you seems to be religious, and bridles not his tongue, but deceives his own heart, this man's religion is vain."

He began to tell the story of a woman he knew while growing up in Chicago. "Sister Trudy wasn't always saved. I knew this woman when she was a thug who would rob you at gunpoint. She wasn't always the woman of God who carried a Bible in one hand and a tract in the other."

Snickering ensued around the sanctuary as Pastor Mullin described his friend.

"Sister Trudy wasn't always the smiling choir member that most members of the old church came to love—this woman whom God loved so much that he took her off the streets of Chicago and gave her a church in which to worship. He put clapping in her hands and running in her feet! The joy of the Lord changed her name from 'Lil Slanga' to 'Woman of God.'"

A round of applause lit up as the members heard the testimony of Sister's Trudy's conversion. Pastor Mullin's paused before continuing. "Now here comes Sister Negativity and Sister Gossipmonger, with their wagging tongues, dripping with death and destruction. They're worried about the wrong things and talk about Sister's Trudy's pantyhose, the way she wears her hair, the way she dresses, and even the shoes on her feet. Learn to bridle that muscle between your cheeks."

Laughter filled the sanctuary again, and people shook their heads in unison.

"Turn with me to Ephesians, chapter four, verse twenty-nine."

Heads bent down as the masses turned the pages of their Bibles.

"Let no corrupt communication proceed out of your mouth but that which is good to the use of edifying, that it may minister grace unto the hearers,' " the pastor recited. He bit his bottom lip as he allowed the scripture to sink in, hoping someone would retain the message.

"If Sister Trudy were still pistol-packing and running the streets of Chicago, I doubt those women would worry much about the color of her panty hose. The way we disrespect each other because we think we can is utterly ridiculous. Some of you are more critical of each other than God. God saw something in this woman that he liked, so he cleaned her up, gave her a new purpose, and placed her among his people. Be not deceived—Sister Trudy may carry the word and a smile, but that sister still packs a nine. So don't be the one to find out just how saved she really is."

Pastor Mullins closed his Bible. "Give God back his house of worship. Allow God's presence to be ushered in with ease, without the presence of strife, back biting and carnal affairs." He looked at the congregation with a look of sorrow "Make a vow to edify your brothers and sisters in the Lord, rather than tear them down with your tongue and misgivings. Be blessed."

Tonya sat next to Carmen, trying to pay attention, but her mind kept wandering to the bathroom conversation she'd overheard concerning Patrick's HIV status. She also thought about how Mary had exposed her health status to her coworkers. She wondered whether anyone at the service knew about this as well. As she scanned the room, she saw a few eyes dart her way then look away.

Why are they looking at me?

"Are you OK?" Carmen whispered.

"I'm fine."

"You're breathing kind of heavily. Would you like me to take you home?"

"No. Don't worry. I'm OK."

Every time the subject of HIV or AIDS came up, Tonya felt both embarrassed and defensive. She once overheard two women in the supermarket discussing the problem of prostitution in the area and how prostitutes were spreading diseases. Tonya could no longer contain herself; she spoke up, despite not having been invited into the conversation.

"Well, they aren't infecting each other. Somebody's buying the product."

"We do have a lot of truck drivers that come through here," one of them said.

"Check your men too," Tonya said, "because I haven't seen any eighteen-wheelers stopping prostitutes."

One of the women rolled her eyes at Tonya and put her hand on her hip. "What are you trying to say? I know my husband don't pick up prostitutes!"

"All I'm saying is that somebody's man is using their service, so we all need to check our homes first before turning our heads and pointing at truck drivers."

"What makes you so sure?"

"If people stopped buying the product, the business would be obsolete."

Not liking what Tonya had to say, the women looked at each other and headed to another aisle.

"Open your eyes, people!" Tonya yelled, as the pair walked away.

Tonya had felt like a hypocrite for speaking one way and thinking another. Just a few months ago, she too had felt the same way. She blamed truck drivers, gay men, prostitutes, and perverted old men for spreading HIV. She never had given these people a face until she'd met a very special, wounded soul at New Covenant Full Gospel.

A young woman who had just moved to town had become a new member of the church. She had brought her two teenage sons with her, and the three were baptized. The woman told a horrific story of being saved from a life of prostitution and abuse and how her former pimp had been arrested a year prior for attempting to kill her. After she was released from the hospital, she took her two children and ran away in fear that he would try to complete the act. She also gave a very shocking account of how, at the age of ten, she had been forced into prostitution by her mother's boyfriend. Her mother had sold her and her sister to her boyfriend for crack. Her sister, who was twelve at the time, ran away but was found by the pimp. She woman never saw her sister again. The woman Tonya now knew as Sister Monique explained that she had contracted HIV from a man when she was only sixteen years old; she was now thirty-two. She remained a prostitute well after contracting HIV. Afraid to stand up to her pimp out of fear for her life, Monique remained a prisoner of the street. She'd found out she was HIV positive when she became pregnant with her third son. She felt guilty for having infected so many unsuspecting men, but she had to make the money or feel the wrath of her pimp's fist. He'd beaten her so badly that one time she ended up in the intensive care unit, fighting for her life.

A tear had rolled down Tonya's face as she had listened to Monique share her story. Her heart went out to her; this woman had endured so much torment in her young life. Tonya admired her for being strong and also being open about her disease. She now realized she could never open up like that, and she wasn't afraid to admit she wasn't nearly as strong as Sister Monique. *As pretty as Monique is, you'd never know she has HIV. She looks as healthy as...as healthy as me,* Tonya thought, as she cried for Monique's sons, who one day might not have their mother. Then she cried for her own child.

Tonya couldn't shake those weird nightmares of her wedding day. Each time she'd wake up right before saying, "I do." In one dream, as she was about to say, "I do," Keith became deathly ill right before her eyes. In another, he ran off with one of the bridesmaids. The dream she'd just had was a repeat of the other dreams, except when the preacher got to the line, "In sickness and in health," Keith turned to her with a needle and syringe filled with tainted blood aimed at her.

Tonya jumped up screaming. Keith, lying beside her, awakened her and tried to comfort her, but the sight of him sent her into a frenzy of emotions. After ten minutes of being awake and realizing it had been a dream, Tonya finally calmed down, but she was still unable to fall back sleep.

What does this mean? Why am I being tormented? Tonya began to question her decision to reconcile her marriage. As if she were in the same room with her, Sister Peggy's voice whispered in her ear*It's just a test. Don't flunk out on God!* She felt at a bit more at ease at the thought of Sister Peggy and her colorful words, which always seemed to make her laugh. She just hoped she was doing the right thing by staying with Keith.

Pastor Mullin was proud of Patrick's recent transformation. He was especially pleased with how he had begun to bring his friends to church, encouraging them to change their lives. One of his friends was the unforgettable Peaches, who came to church dressed in a bright-yellow suit, a white shirt, a yellow tie, and a pair of bone-colored snakeskin shoes. His getup reminded Tonya of 1940s zoot suits. His clothes seemed to be two sizes too big, and he looked to be underweight by thirty pounds. At five feet nine inches tall, he weighed a shocking 102 pounds. Peaches's hair was a head full of twists and locks. He had his eyebrows waxed and his nails manicured with French tips and wore a couple of layers of makeup, much like Patrick had before he had converted his life by accepting Christ into his heart. He had stopped demanding others call his Patricia, no longer dressed or acted as a woman. Patrick has spoken to Pastor Mullins and had shared some eye opening information with him. At a young age he was molested by a neighbor's son, Jordan, who was much older than he. The sexual act confused young Patrick, who began to believe that it was common and acceptable for boys to engage in this manner with other boys. He never told a soul, until that very moment while sitting in Pastor's Mullin's office. The older boy who introduced Patrick to this lifestyle groomed him to this new world. He took Patrick to private parties held in hotel rooms, clubs or someone's home. Jordan was sixteen and young Patrick was ten when the two first met. Initially, Jordan showed Patrick how to dress, keep his hair and nails neat and how to maintain good posture. The older boy hung out with the younger Patrick very often. Sister White thought it was good for Patrick to have such an older boy finding interest in him. Patrick maintained his grades in school, not alarming his mother that anything outside the norm was taking place. By the time Patrick was twelve, he had seen the secret life the Jordan lived. He liked the clubs, music, and the excitement of knowing something no one else knew. He felt convicted of having sex with a man, but he eventually buried those feelings of guilt and lived his life as he wanted. By the time Patrick for sixteen, Jordan cut him loose. He was no longer interested in the mature Patrick. Jordan had his eyes on a much younger thirteen year old newcomer, Cody. Cody's family had moved three houses down from Patrick. He had seen the boy walking with his dog, a black Cockier Spaniard. He didn't have the same interest in young boys as Jordan, but Patrick knew that once Jordan had his eyes on young Cody, he was his for the taking. Patrick was left lost and confused after Jordan lost interest in him, leaving him to fend for himself. Patrick felt as if he was pushed aside and left standing in the rain. Over the next five years, Patrick tried to find himself, but felt it was best to just reinvent himself as Patricia. He could have saved himself a lot of heartache and trouble if he had realized earlier that Jordan wasn't attracted to him because he was special nor did he leave him because he'd done anything wrong. Jordan was a pedophile, he was only interested in Patrick's youth and when Patrick had outgrown his desired age, he moved on to younger prey. He shared with Pastor Mullin how he was hurt and confused and how he just wanted to find the little boy who used to sing in the choir, attend Sunday school and love life. Patrick cried and asked God for forgiveness. It was the first time in over ten years that he has felt convicted of his sins. He knew at that moment that God had heard him and that he had not left his heart. Patrick sat in the church service praying that God would give his good friend Peaches the same peace that he'd found.

Peaches' eyes were a pair of dull marbles, with no sparkle left in them. Although he wore makeup, his skin was patchy and dry. It would be fair to say that he resembled the alien from *Men in Black* that had slipped into a human's skin.

During the Sunday service, Peaches laughed and pointed at Sister Peggy and other members as they rejoiced during the worship service. When Sister Peggy felt the spirit, it was obvious to anyone within hearing distance that Peaches thought this was a comedy show.

"Tell your friend to keep his voice down!" Sister White whispered into Patrick's ear, after watching Peaches all but roll on the floor laughing.

"It's his first time here."

"That makes no never mind."

"Yes, ma'am."

Leaning toward Peaches, Patrick whispered, "Hey, keep it down! This is my mother's church."

The scene during the altar call also was uncomfortable. Peaches sat with his arms and legs crossed, revealing his matching yellow socks.

"I am fab-u-lous, honey. I don't need anyone telling me I'm not!" he snapped when encouraged to give his life to God.

One of the ushers pressed a finger to her lips as a gesture for Peaches to be quiet.

"Oh, no, she didn't! I am about to set it off up in here!" Turning to Patrick as if he didn't believe what had just occurred, he said, "Did sistah girl just shush me?"

"Please don't disrespect the house of the Lord. You can do that in the club but not in here," Patrick advised Peaches, clearly embarrassed by his behavior.

Offended that Patrick didn't take his side, Peaches turned his body away from him by crossing his legs and shifting his hip in his seat. He folded his bony arms across his chest and poked his lips out like a kid.

"Keep praying for him," Sister White encouraged Patrick.

Patrick watched Peaches apply another coat of makeup to his already heavily powdered face. He noticed his friend's physical appearance had begun to deteriorate along with his health.

Peaches was beginning to show increased signs of advanced stages of the disease. He was no longer the hyperactive young man Patrick had known for seven years. He walked at a slower pace and with little energy. Although he had lost a tremendous amount of weight, his abdomen protruded. His eyes were as yellow as the socks he wore, which were indicative of jaundice secondary to hepatitis C. Peaches was always flamboyant in everything he did, but the disease had even curbed that aspect of him. A year ago Peaches would have done more than pout; he would have turned the whole service out. Patrick could only do what his mother suggested, "Keep praying for him."

That was Patrick's last Sunday attending church services. The following week he became increasingly weak. Sister White religiously sat at his bedside, feeding him and administering his medication and respiratory treatments. Patrick had been down this road before, and each time it took a little more out of him.

Tonya always had made it a habit to visit the sick and shut-ins, but due to the circumstances of her own condition, she elected to call instead. She couldn't put herself or her baby in harm's way. She used her pregnancy as an excuse for not visiting Patrick when she found out that he was again bedridden. During the phone conversation with Sister White, Tonya began to doubt her own faith. How could she truly believe Patrick would overcome this bout of pneumonia when he was so weak and fragile?

This time was different. Patrick had decided to quit his antiretroviral medication. His already compromised immune system welcomed a deadly case of meningitis that ravaged his body.

"He's going to beat this," Sister White announced when Tonya called her.

"How's he doing?"

"Not well, but he'll get better. I know he will."

"Sure he will!" Tonya added, not believing her own words.

"The prayer of the righteous availeth much."

"Amen." Tonya said halfheartedly. How could Patrick stop taking his medication? It was the only thing that had kept him well this long. After she quickly hung up the phone with Sister White, it dawned on her that maybe Patrick was tired of the fight.

33

The ringing phone woke Tonya. Annoyed, she turned over and pulled the covers over her head. Keith reached for the phone and mumbled, "Hello?"

"Wait, slow down…" After a few seconds of listening to the caller, he tugged at Tonya in an attempt to wake her.

"Tonya! It's Sister Peggy. She sounds upset."

Opening her eyes at the sound of Sister's Peggy's name, Tonya sat up in bed. "Hello?" she asked, sounding panicked. She heard crying and screaming in the background.

"He's gone! My baby's gone!"

"Tonya, I hate to call you at such an ungodly hour," Sister Peggy said, "but I'm at Sister White's house. I could really use your support because she just lost her son."

Sister Betty, a neighbor of Sister White, took the phone from Sister Peggy to give Tonya the message. Sister Betty stated that she couldn't handle both the grieving Sister White and Sister Peggy and needed Tonya's assistance.

"I'm on my way!" Tonya said, jumping out of bed with Keith in tow.

Sister White arranged to have the funeral a week after Patrick's death, which allowed the family from out of town to attend. Sister White's adopted twin siblings, Tracy and Raheem, came together. Their mother wasn't in attendance because she was too sick to travel, and their father had passed away five years earlier. Patrick's father wasn't expected to attend the funeral. He had walked out of Patrick's life when he had learned that he was gay and transgender.

Patrick was seventeen years old when he told his father he wanted to live his life as a woman. His father backhanded him across the face and told him to get out of his house, informing him that he no longer had a son. This was crushing to Patrick's ego, but he refused to cry. He had been ridiculed by kids at school, people in his neighborhood, and even people at church, but he never thought his dad would be one of them. He never played football, basketball, or any contact sports. He was more interested in fashion design and makeup. Sister White thought it was just a phase, but that phase lasted well into adulthood.

Tracy and Raheem were adopted by Sister White's parents when she was fifteen and the twins were two years old. The twins had come from an abusive family. Their mother was addicted to crack cocaine and couldn't care for her toddlers. She often left the children home alone to get a quick fix. Her quick runs turned into hours that then turned into days. The twins were left in the house for four days before the neighbors called the police. They reported that they hadn't seen the mother in a few days but heard the children crying constantly. When the twins were rescued, they were hungry, dehydrated, and dirty. Social services stepped in and took the children from their mother. A year later Sister White had two new siblings.

The twins remained close, living together in their own apartment while struggling through college. They were mirror images of each other but opposite in every other way. Raheem's major had been engineering. He was always more intellectual than his sister. Tracy had majored in early-childhood education. Her grades were average, whereas Raheem had excelled in school. Tracy was more athletic and had played softball, volleyball, and basketball. Raheem had been on the debate team and was a member of the science and math club, which kept his mind challenged.

Because of the age difference between the twins and Sister White, Tracy and Raheem often looked up to her as a mother figure. They'd kept in touch with her over the years and were both were very fond of Patrick. He wasn't much younger than the twins, so naturally they interacted well with one another. Tracy took Patrick's death especially hard, because she viewed him as a second brother.

When Tracy mentioned the idea of having Patrick cremated, Sister White dramatically clutched her chest, as if she were having a heart attack.

"I could never do that to my child! I need to know he's resting in a deep sleep, not burned and sitting in some cup!"

Patrick was dressed in a dark-purple suit with a matching tie and handkerchief. His hair was cut short, since most of it had fallen out during his illness. On his right hand was his class ring; he had been so proud of it.

"He looks so peaceful," Sister White told the twins as she stood before Patrick's casket.

"I hate seeing him like this. He was always so full of life." Tracy reached over and gently stroked Patrick's face.

"It's a shame he died at such a young age."

The trio turned around to see who had spoken these words.

Patrick's dad stood behind them with a strained look on his face.

"I…uh…I didn't expect to see you here," Sister White said, stumbling over her words.

"He's still my son, no matter what," Patrick's father said.

"I thought you no longer had a son." The bitterness she felt for her husband was evident in her voice.

"I was wrong for kicking him out of my life, but I didn't think it would be the last time I would see him."

"Well, your 'sorry' don't matter now. It won't bring him back, and he can't hear it no way."

"I know…I just wish he knew I still loved him. What man wants to raise his son and be told that he didn't raise him well enough to be the kind of man he'd hoped for?"

"Patrick was your flesh and blood," Sister White said, "regardless of how he lived. I loved him even before he found his way back home. All he needed was love. You don't throw away your children, even if they don't meet your expectations."

"I know that too. I just wished I hadn't waited so long to tell him I was sorry." Mr. White's voiced cracked as he dropped his head in shame.

Sister White's face softened a bit. "He forgave you a long time ago. He just wanted you to accept him."

"I couldn't, but I'm glad he turned his life around, even if it was too late."

"It wasn't too late. He's in a better place now. I prayed every night for my child—that's what mothers do— and God brought him back to me," Sister White said, idly straightening her son's already neat suit.

34

The day of Patrick's funeral was rainy, dark, and gloomy. It was as if heaven had opened up and cried. Patrick was a quiet storm in life, so it was only natural for there to be a quiet period after his death. It was as if the sun had refused to shine on this particular day. The angels rejoiced for having him onboard, for he too was one of God's angels. They knew that it broke his mother's heart to lose her beloved son.

Sister White wasn't herself; she was a walking zombie—a medicated and unemotional walking zombie. She had spent the past five days trying to plan the perfect funeral for Patrick, as if there was such a thing. The smallest details were repeatedly questioned. The tie clip had fingerprints on it, so it had to be wiped with a clean handkerchief. His class ring had to be cleaned before it was put back on his finger before the funeral. His nails had to be clipped and painted with clear polish that gave them a shine. Those were the kind of things that didn't matter to those who mourned his passing, but to Sister White they were the most important tasks at hand. She had to do whatever she could for him, since it would be the last time she'd be able to do her motherly duties.

Tonya had cradled her belly as she thought about her love for her unborn child. "Sister White, you're going to burn yourself out. Let me help you with the arrangements," she had suggested to her.

"I'm fine. I don't feel tired at all."

"Your 'not feeling' is the problem. You've got to grieve."

"I have a lifetime to grieve. Right now I have to bury my son."

Tonya knew Sister White would fall like a building during a demolition once things were over. She had been up cooking, cleaning, and fussing over

Patrick since he had passed. She refused to accept any help, believing only she knew what Patrick would have wanted.

My guess is not to be dead, Tonya thought when Sister White asked what she thought Patrick would want during his funeral.

Family and friends filed to Sister's white's house to show their support with words of encouragement. One by one they hugged her and promised to be there for her during this trying time. Some offered stories of Patrick and his antics, which took everyone's mind off the sad moment. One of Patrick's friends, a young man by name of Juan hugged Sister White. He looked to be no older than twenty-two years old. "Momma White, I will miss Patrick the most. We had a close relationship over the past eight years. He was there for me when my 'friend' died. Patrick was a good person and I will miss him dearly." Juan had dated an older man who knowingly had HIV, but he promised Juan that he would take care of him when he died. Juan cared for the man, even when he was too incapacitated to get out of bed. Juan was his care giver, friend and lover til the end, even sacrificing his own health. His friend, who was married, but estranged, from his wife and three children left Juan to live in the house that they'd shared for the past five years. When the man's wife got wind of Juan, she quickly evicted him, closed the bank account and left him to fend for himself. Juan turned to Patrick for help. Patrick helped Juan find a place to live with some of his underground friends. Patrick's underground friends were people in high places who lived the lifestyle, but did so in secrecy. They were lawyers, doctors, executives, athletes and even some big time preachers who ventured that way. Juan was set up in a nice apartment that was paid for by a success-ful attorney. He had only one condition for Juan, he could only be with him. He didn't believe in sharing, and he didn't like to flaunt his sexuality around. Juan quickly agreed. Juan was always grateful for Patrick's help. He never told Patrick that was infected as well. Juan never told a soul.

Pastor Mullin made it a point to address the highlights of Patrick's life. The eulogy was quick, since Patrick had just begun to live. Sister White was very composed, mostly due to the sedative she'd taken that morning. It took both her husband and her brother to keep her in an upright position.

The funeral lasted only an hour. Not many of Patrick's friends came, not even Peaches, who was too ill to attend. He had called to say he wished he could be there to give his final respects, but he'd probably see Patrick soon enough. Peaches had confined himself to his home, not wanting anyone to see him in such a feeble state. His premonition proved to be correct; he passed away two months later.

Tracy and Raheem performed beautifully, singing a duo of "Amazing Grace," Patrick's favorite song. A few of Patrick's friends who did attend, stood t share accounts of how he was such a good friend and how he would be sorely missed. They promised to be there for Sister White, but isn't that what everybody say? Jordan did not attend the funeral and his absence was noticeable. Sister White had seen him as Patrick's mentor. Growing up, the two were inseparable, why hadn't Jordan come around? Even during her grief, she'd never forgotten about how Jordan had cared for her son.

Pastor Mullin's eulogy was followed by one last viewing, during which Sister White gave her son one last kiss.

Just as quickly as it had begun, it was over.

35

"Tonya, baby, wake up!" Keith said, nudging her playfully.

"Huh? What's wrong?"

"We're going to be late for church."

Tonya couldn't believe her ears. "You're going to church?"

"Yeah, I think it's about time."

"Oh, Keith. I'm so happy!" she squealed, embracing him.

"Chop, chop! Let's get going," Keith said with a smile.

It had been a long time since he had attended church. He even had stopped going on special occasions, such as Easter and Mother's Day, but he knew he had to turn his life around to give his marriage half a chance. Tonya constantly had tried to encourage him to attend church with her; now it was up to him to take responsibility for the salvation of his soul.

With a towel wrapped around her body, she stepped out of the shower. Keith stood at the bathroom sink, shaving his overgrown beard. Tonya noticed specks of red mixed with his shaving cream, where he'd nicked himself. Keith had neglected his haircuts and shaves at the barber since he had found out about his HIV status.

"When are you going to get your hair cut? You're beginning to look like a mountain man."

Looking at his reflection in the mirror, Keith acknowledged his rugged appearance and desperate need for a haircut. "I'll have it cut soon. I can't cut my own hair, but it really needs to be done. I'll look into it. Do you think it's safe?"

"People get haircuts all the time. They do sanitize the equipment. Surely you can't get blood transfer from clippers—can you?" The question hung in the air; Keith didn't have an answer.

Tonya's question stayed with him as he got dressed. *How many times are people exposed to other people's blood?* he wondered. Getting a haircut at the barbershop, getting a manicure, getting a tattoo, or getting a piercing—these were all potentially deadly exchanges.

—⁂—

The thought of having to sit in the same row as Carmen made Keith feel uncomfortable. She'd held so much animosity toward him since he and Tonya had separated months ago. Despite their reconciliation, Carmen didn't let up on him. Throughout the service, Carmen gave Keith hateful glares.

"Why are you so hard on Keith?" Tonya asked, after noticing her menacing stares.

"He's done the unforgivable. Why aren't you angry with him?"

"If I can forgive him, why can't you?"

"You're too soft, Tonya. You need to grow a backbone."

"Forgiveness takes backbone. It takes more strength to forgive than to walk around with anger in your heart."

"I still think you can do better than to accept what's been dealt to you."

"First Peter, chapter three, verse nine tells us not to repay evil for evil but to repay with blessings."

Carmen didn't understand Tonya's theory or her decision to stay with Keith *Peter's wife didn't give him HIV*, she thought then turned her attention to the service and Pastor Mullin's rendition of Martin Luther King Jr.'s famous speech "How Long? Not Long!"

Keith seemed to enjoy the service; he especially enjoyed when the choir sang one of Tonya's favorite songs, Hezekiah Walker's "Faithful Is Our God." Keith stood up and raised his hands in praise as he sang along with the choir, "I'm reaping the harvest God promised me."

Feeling a flutter in her stomach, Tonya placed a hand on her abdomen to calm her baby as the choir sang. Carmen looked at her and smiled. "I think he likes this song." Tonya caressed her belly as the baby jumped with joy. The baby was beginning to become more active, often keeping Tonya awake at night.

The church was alive as the choir sang. Tonya looked around the sanctuary and took in the sight of God's people in praise and worship; the church was in full swing. She needed to feel God's spirit this morning. She knew God was present as she saw everyone praising and worshiping. Tonya hummed along to the song—"The presence of the Lord is here. The presence of the Lord is here. I feel it in the atmosphere. Oh, the presence of the Lord is here."

A few rows back, she spotted a group of small children, who looked to be no more than three or four years old, imitating their elders. A little girl dressed in pink and white with matching hair bows jumped around, throwing her hands in the air as she took a dive to the floor. Tonya immediately recognized that to be Sister Peggy. The little girl's playmates each took a role, imitating different church members. Tonya laughed as she watched. A little boy had Pastor Mullin down to a T, as he marched around with a church fan held upside down, using it as a microphone. He wiped the sweat from his brow, formed a large O with his mouth, and leaned back as he preached. Tonya imagined her own child growing up at New Covenant and imitating parishioners. *Raise a child up in the way that he should go*, she thought.

During the sermon Keith sat alert and focused. He gave Pastor Mullin his undivided attention, only looking at Tonya when the pastor requested an occasional, "Turn to your neighbor and say…"

36

The following Sunday, feeling emotionally and physically drained, Tonya spent the entire day in bed. She ignored the ringing telephone along with her husband's request to accompany him to church.

"I can't make it this morning. Tell Sister Peggy I'll call her later."

"Sure, just get some rest," Keith said, worried that Tonya could be really sick and not have told him.

The following morning the words on the computer screen merged as Tonya sat in front of her laptop. Feeling a headache coming on, she decided to take a break.

"These dizzy spells are occurring more often. I'm not able to get much work done," Tonya reported to Carmen the next day.

"Maybe you should call your doctor. Your face has been looking kind of swollen lately. Is that normal?"

"I don't know what's normal anymore. This pregnancy is different than most pregnancies. I have more medical problems than most women. Maybe I'll go see the doctor tomorrow. It's too late to go in today."

"Tonya, it's only nine o'clock. They're just opening. Just go and get checked out. I'll drive you."

Reluctantly Tonya agreed.

The nurse greeted Tonya as she led her behind the office door. Her vital signs were taken, along with her weight. She had gained ten pounds since her last doctor's appointment two weeks ago, and her blood pressure was excessively high, which alarmed Dr. Gipson.

"Mrs. Paris, I'm very concerned about your blood pressure, weight gain, and generalized edema. I'd like for you to be admitted to the hospital for observation."

"For how long?" she asked. "I don't particularly like hospitals."

"Until those problems are resolved and I'm satisfied that both mother and baby aren't in danger."

—⁂—

After rapping lightly on the door, Carmen entered the hospital room to see Tonya reclined in bed, watching TV. Carrying a bouquet of freshly cut flowers, she put on a brave face for her sister.

"Hey, girl! I thought I'd make your day by letting you see this beautiful face," Carmen teased.

"Vanity of vanity. All is vanity!"

Rolling her eyes, Carmen retorted, "You always bring everything back to the Bible!"

Crossing the room, Carmen gave her sister a hug then placed the flowers in the windowsill. She took a seat next to Tonya's bed, crossed her legs, and gave her sister a stern look. "I hope you haven't been sitting here worrying about anything," she said. Things are going to be fine. You've just got to stop letting Keith get on your nerves. In fact he's probably the reason you're here."

"Please don't start on Keith. He's doing so much better since we got back together."

"Fine, fine. I don't want to upset you."

Changing the subject, Carmen turned her attention to the television. "I know you're not watching one of those baby-daddy shows!"

"I'm not watching TV at all. It's more like the TV is watching me. I'd rather be at home in my own bed."

"You'll be home as soon as your blood pressure stabilizes. Just get some rest. Lord knows you need it."

Tonya stroked her belly. "How do they think I can get any rest in a strange place? The staff comes in every five minutes to take vital signs and ask questions, and they make so much noise. 'Dr. Thomas, call the operator. Code red, white, and blue.' It's all so unnerving."

"We both know that if you were home, rest is the last thing you'd be getting."

Retrieving a hairbrush and comb from her purse, Carmen ordered, "Now move over and let me get a hold of your head. You look like a throwed away child." She began to sing in the tune of an old Negro spiritual, "Sometimes I feel like a throwed-away child…"

"Shut up already, and do my hair before I put you out!"

"Yes, your highness!" Carmen laughed as she brushed her sister's hair.

Members of New Covenant visited, bringing Tonya good news about the Sunday school, the service, or some form of gossip, all dressed up in a prayer request. Sister Peggy showed up, colorful as ever. "Chile, Pastor Mullin really preached the word! The devil had me, but God sot me loose."

Giggling to herself, Tonya interpreted the message as, "The devil had me, but God set me loose." Sister Peggy preached the message, giving her spin to it, and danced around the room. She made so much noise that the nurse had to ask her to keep it down or leave. She humbly sat down, just long enough to say a quick prayer before leaving.

"Just be strong and know that by his stripes you're healed. You believe it, and God's gonna do it. Just you believe. He's a healer, and he can do anything but fail, so rise up like Lazareth!"

"Sister Peggy, I'm not dead, just here for observation," Tonya joked. "Thanks for your words of comfort, and please keep me in your prayers."

"You're always in my prayers."

Giving her a quick peck on the cheek, Sister Peggy patted her hand and left the room.

Lying in bed all day made Tonya depressed. She wasn't one to lie around bored. *Lord, I need you now*, she prayed. *This hospital isn't where I need to be. This is for those I visit weekly, not me.* Feeling restless, she turned on the television. As she changed the channels, she felt lost. She never watched T.V during the daytime, "There's nothing on but soap operas and game shows and 'Who's my baby daddy?' shows," Tonya mumbled, as she turned the volume down low. She resisted turning the television off, as she needed some stimulation in her empty room. Resting her head on the pillows, she closed her eyes and recalled various memories from her life. First she envisioned her favorite people from her childhood. Faces came into her mental view as she thought about those characters during different stages of her life. Two people who stood out were old members of New Covenant, Mother Smith and Elder Sloan.

Tonya reflected on Sister Peggy's deceased mother, Mother Betty Jean Smith. Having no more than a sixth-grade education, Mother Smith had taught every member of the church one or more of her God-given messages. The members of the church would ignite the fire in Mother Smith with a simple request—"Mother, I need a word from the Lord."

Mother Smith, whether sitting or standing, would lean on her cane and moan a little before she gave the word that the Lord had for that particular person at that particular time, all the while rocking to her own beat.

"Well, chile, you know the Lawd is almighty, and if the Lawd can't do it, it can't get dunt, and if the Lawd can't fix it, it can't get fix, and if the Lawd can't give it, it can't get got, and if the Lawd can't heal it, it can't get healt. So just you believe, chile. Believe that the Lawd is almighty and he can do anythang but fail!"

Tears formed in Tonya's eyes as she laughed at how Mother Smith had passed on her ways to her daughter. Sister Peggy was certainly her mother's daughter.

Elder Logan also was from the old church, where the phrase "A woman should be seen and not heard" was spoken on a daily basis. He made it a point to prowl around the church, lurking in corners in order to spot the women acting unladylike. His wife was just as bad; carried a handkerchief in one hand and the Bible in the other. Sister Logan believed that a proper woman always carried a handkerchief, which she spread across her lap while sitting in church. The idea behind this was to cover your rising skirt or dress once seated, but her dresses always fell below her knees. It was based on principle alone.

One Sunday morning, while the choir was preparing to march in to sing the pastor's all-time favorite song, "Do Not Pass Me By," the women were standing in hallway when someone in the soprano section started to sing.

Elder Logan jumped out from his hiding place. "Ladies, keep the noise down. You should conduct yourself in a ladylike manner!"

"Oh, I'm sorry for being so loud. I just love this song."

Elder Logan's face went from brown to ashen gray when he realized the loud soprano was none other than Patrick White. Elder Logan stammered, "Keep it down…uh…son," before turning on his heels.

The choir's giggles didn't help shield his embarrassment. He was mortified. It was good to see him get what was coming.

Tonya smiled at the memory of Elder Logan. "Bless his soul," she uttered, as she thought about the fallen soldier. *Some real characters have come through New Covenant.*

37

Rushing to be at Tonya's side as she prepared to give birth to their son, Keith entered the hospital without so much as acknowledging the hospital volunteers standing near the entrance.

"Sir, would you like to make a donation to the Children's Hospital?"

Keith approached the information desk, where two smiling elderly volunteers were handing out coloring books and crayons to a couple of children. Without giving them time to finish what he thought was an irrelevant greeting, Keith interrupted. "Can you tell me where I can find my wife? She's here to give birth to my son!"

One of the ladies turned to Keith and cheerfully congratulated him on becoming a father, then directed him to the labor-and-delivery unit. Walking past the gift shop, Keith noticed a display of balloons, T-shirts, door ornaments, and banners reading, "It's a Boy!" or "It's a Girl!" He thought about getting something for his son but decided against it for the moment; he didn't want to keep Tonya or his son waiting any longer.

He had gotten a call at work, telling him to come to the hospital because Tonya had gone into labor. This came as a great surprise to him since she wasn't due for another twelve weeks. Keith was so excited that he hadn't realized that Tonya's giving birth this early could be devastating to both her and the baby.

After he made his way up to the labor-and-delivery unit, he approached the nurses' station and asked if they could direct him to Tonya Paris's room. The nurse, a thin redheaded woman who looked to be around twenty-five, emerged from behind the desk and escorted him to Tonya's room.

"Sir, your wife is being given medication to stop the birth," the nurse said. "She's too early."

"It's just a few weeks. What does that matter?"

"Sir, twelve weeks isn't just a few weeks to a premature fetus."

"Well, what if she has the baby today?"

"We'd have to take the baby to the NICU," the nurse said, referring to the Neonatal Intensive Care Unit.

"Then do it! As long as our son is born today!"

The nurse looked at Keith with an annoyed expression. He clearly didn't understand the consequences of such a premature birth.

"Sir, your son will be very sick if he's born too early."

"Oh, well, what are you doing to stop that?"

"We'll do everything we can, but it's up to the baby. Sometimes they come when they want to—there's no stopping them."

As Keith entered the room, he saw Tonya lying in bed. She looked so frail and drained. "Hey, are you all right?" he said, as he approached her. "You don't look too good."

Tonya's voice was just above a whisper. "I'm not doing well. I can't keep my blood pressure down, and the medicine they're giving me makes me sick and dizzy."

Keith took in the nicely decorated room, which gave him the feeling of being at home. The wall was covered with soothing pictures of doves, swans, and seagulls; he saw a monitor with a long slip of graph paper that was steadily printing out of the slot. He didn't know what it was recording, but the nurse seemed very interested in it. After noticing Keith's puzzled look, she explained the lines and numbers on the machine. In the corner of the room, he noticed Carmen sitting in a chair. The look on her face was one of sheer hate.

"She's sick," Carmen said. "Oh, but you knew that already."

"Hi, Carmen. I didn't see you sitting there."

Another nurse entered the room, headed to the monitor, and read the strips as they flowed from the machine. She walked over to the IV pump and hung a small bag next to the large bag of fluid already there. Then she pushed a button on the monitor that took Tonya's vital signs, jotted them down, then dipped a cloth into a basin of water and placed the cloth on Tonya's forehead.

"Mrs. Paris, we've got to get your blood pressure down," she said. "I'll be back to check on you in a little while. Try to get some rest." As she prepared to leave, she paused at the foot of Tonya's bed. She pulled the sheet back to reveal a pair of very puffy and swollen feet. Then she placed her index finger on Tonya's foot and pushed down. "I'll be back shortly," she said, as she exited the room.

"OK. Thanks," Tonya replied weakly.

—◊◊—

Those dreams of her wedding day came back to haunt her once more. *As she walked down the aisle, escorted by her father, she saw Keith, Carmen, and Pastor Mullin standing at the altar…but why would her mother be here? Bethany Lacey stood smiling at her daughter. She was dressed in a beautiful white dress, her hair pinned up like she always wore it when Tonya was a little girl. Everyone stood smiling at Tonya, as if Bethany Lacey was supposed to be there.*

"What is she doing here?" Tonya asked Elder Lacey.

"Who, dear?"

"Mom. Why is Mom here?"

"It's your wedding day, honey. Everyone's invited." He smiled at Tonya as he let go of her hand.

Bethany Lacey stepped forward, grabbed Tonya by the hand, and led her toward the altar, past Keith, Pastor Mullin, and Carmen. Her mother's face looked so serene; her angelic smile put Tonya at ease. She no longer felt confused or fearful, as she walked hand in hand with her long-departed mother.

As Tonya lay in bed, her face appeared puffy, and her hands looked as if they might burst open, which made Keith concerned.

"What's going on with you?" he said. "You look terrible. What's up with all these IV tubes?"

Tonya didn't respond.

"When's the doctor going to get here?"

Still no response.

Carmen jumped up and crossed the room "Tonya? Tonya!" she yelled.

Tonya's body was rigid, her eyes open, mouth closed, and teeth clamped tightly on her tongue.

Blood dripped from the corner of her mouth "Tonya!" Carmen yelled, shaking her. Suddenly the machines blared loudly, indicating something was seriously wrong. Turning to Keith, Carmen screamed, "Get the nurse. She's having a seizure!"

Sprinting full speed out of the room, Keith ran to find help. As he approached the nurses' station, he realized no one was sitting there. *Fine time to take a break!* He ran down the hallway and spotted a nurse coming out of a patient's room. "Hey," he said, "my wife needs help!"

As a herd of nurses and doctors rushed into the room, Keith and Carmen were bumped and pushed aside. The staff finally asked them to step outside the room.

Pacing the floor, Carmen couldn't put the pieces together. One minute Tonya was talking; the next she was unresponsive and having a seizure. What had gone wrong? As she stood outside her sister's room, she felt helpless. She pulled out her cell phone and called her dad; he'd know what to do.

Carmen hysterically cried into the phone as she tried to fill her father in on what had just happened to Tonya. All he could make out was Tonya's name between Carmen's screams and sobs. He tried to yell over her screams, but to no avail. He was getting nowhere with trying to get information from her. "I'm on my way," he said through clenched teeth. He quickly hung up the phone and headed to the hospital. He tightly gripped the steering wheel as he made sharp turns, ran through yellow caution lights and slid through stop signs, praying all the way. He prayed that Tonya would hold on until he got to the hospital. He didn't get a clear understanding from Carmen, only that Tonya has taken a turn for the worse and was whisked away to the operating room for an emergency cesarean section.

He began to reflect on years ago when he had lost his wife. That was the darkest time in his life. He had never felt so lost or so alone. He had no idea how he would be able to raise two young girls by himself. Bethany had always done everything for the girls. She kept their hair neatly combed, clothes nicely pressed, dinner on the table and the house tidy. When she became ill, he felt lost. How could he do the things that she had done to keep the family together?

Pulling up to the parking lot of the hospital, he jumped out of the car, forgetting to lock it as he sprinted away. He mumbled a militant prayer for strength, reminding God of his promise, "Lord, you said that the righteous cry and you hear, and deliver them out of their trouble. Well, Lord I am troubled."

A small still voice spoke to him, "She's my righteous servant as well. She is in need of deliverance from her trouble. Be ready."

Elder Lacey   stood still as this revelation sank in, his heart quickened its pace as realization set in, with a sense of calm. He felt a sudden shift in the atmosphere. He increased his pace as he rushed to be at Carmen's side. She would need him now.

The staff wouldn't let them back in to see Tonya, but Carmen noticed that a lot of people were coming in and out of the room. Why wouldn't someone stop long enough to tell them something?

"What's going on with my sister?" Carmen asked a young lady who looked as scared as she did.

"I'm not authorized to speak to the family, but I'll get someone for you," she said, disappearing back inside the room.

Suddenly the door flew open, and doctors, nurses, and staff in blue scrubs were wheeling Tonya down the hall. An oxygen mask covered her face. A nurse pumped a round bag attached to the facemask as they wheeled her down the hall. No one stopped to explain what they were doing or where they were taking her.

Everything was such a blur; it took mere seconds before they were out of view behind a steel door that read, Personnel Only. Carmen waited until someone finally came out to speak to the family. The nurse explained that Tonya had to be taken to surgery for an emergency C-section. Things were happening so fast that neither Carmen nor Keith could comprehend the situation.

When the doctor came to speak to the family, Carmen knew before he opened his mouth. The room spun as the man dressed in blue surgical garb approached. The terse look on his face told it all.

Carmen could focus only on one thing. "Where's my sister? Where's my sister?" she yelled. She let out a bloodcurdling scream as the doctor confirmed her deepest fear.

38

Carmen sat in the front church pew, staring at her sister's beautiful, unsmiling, still face, and her newborn nephew, who never experienced life, forever sleeping with his mother. She was grief stricken. How could someone so kind, sweet, and loving be taken before her time?

Tonya was laid to rest in a cream-colored dress with a blue-satin sash that matched her baby's blue-satin outfit. The baby, whom Tonya had wanted to name Cameron, was too small to survive his early birth; his lungs were just too underdeveloped. Despite the emergency cesarean section, baby Cameron didn't survive his journey. Tonya never recovered from the multiple seizures; the doctors said it was preeclampsia, caused by her extremely high blood pressure. Once she'd started having seizures, she'd lost oxygen to her brain, and the baby also was deprived of oxygen during that time. Tonya never got the chance to see her precious baby boy, whom Carmen thought looked just like her. Tears rolled down Carmen's cheeks as she placed her face against her father's chest. "Daddy, I never even got a chance to say good-bye."

Even in his own grief-stricken state, Elder Lacey comforted the only family he had left.

Out of the corner of her eye, Carmen saw Keith and became even more furious. As if some entity possessed her body, she leapt to her feet and attacked Keith, swinging her fists in rage and screaming, "Murderer! Why are you here? You can't kill her anymore. You can't hurt her anymore! You murdered my sister. You should be in prison for what you did. Better yet, you should be mutilated, castrated, then decapitated for your crime. You should be the one lying here. My sister deserved better. She didn't deserve this, you, you…"

Keith stood still, allowing Carmen to attack him, both physically and verbally. He felt guilty, responsible, and rightfully the source of her anger. He couldn't bring back his family, nor could he change places with them. If he could, he would do so without hesitation.

Elder Lacey grabbed Carmen and held her in his arms as she cried. Brian and Jerry came to Keith's rescue and led him away from his hysterical sister-in-law.

Overcome with grief and rage, Carmen suddenly felt her legs betray her, and she sank to the floor, sobbing uncontrollably. She wished she could bargain with God to bring her sister back, but she knew it was too late. She felt her father's arms around her as he picked her up from the floor. She allowed him to cradle her in his embrace.

"Daddy, why Tonya? Why, Daddy? Why?"

Elder Lacey had no answers for her, because secretly, just a little while ago, he too had questioned his faith in God. How could someone so sweet and loving suffer from an illness not caused by her but by someone she'd entrusted to love and cherish her? She was a God-fearing woman who had served the church faithfully. Why did this have to happen to her? Even so, he knew she was in better place now.

"Baby girl, she's in the arms of the Lord and will shed no more tears, because once again God has made her whole."

Carmen took solace in her father's words, a man who had suffered the same loss but whose outlook was totally different from hers. Instead of anger he found peace in knowing that as much as Tonya loved God, God loved her that much more. Carmen just hadn't reached that point yet.

When the time came for the family to speak a word on behalf of Tonya, Carmen wanted to show those who didn't know her sister who she really was. Her voice trembled with emotion as she read the poem she had written for her sister's birthday when she was twelve and Tonya was fifteen. Carmen reflected on the day she had given Tonya the poem and how she had hugged her and they had cried together.

My Sister and Friend
You held me when I wept.
You held me when I slept
Now that Mom is gone,

you stepped in right on time.
You showed me love when I was lonely
and protected me when I was scared.
You are my hero, my big sister, and my best friend.

As Carmen read the poem, she knew Tonya's spirit was embracing her as she cried. She realized she'd never be able to hold or be held by her sister again, at least not in this lifetime.

She walked up to the pink-and-white casket that held her sister and newborn nephew. She took the gold bracelet she'd had engraved a few months earlier and placed it on her sister's wrist. She wanted Tonya to always have it as a token of her love.

Pastor Mullin spoke about the joy of dying in Christ, but Carmen felt nothing close to joy. "O death, where is thy sting? O grave, where is thy victory? The sting of death is sin, and the strength of sin is the law. But thanks be to God, which giveth us the victory through our Lord Jesus Christ." Pastor Mullin snatched a handkerchief off the podium in front of him, took a deep breath, then looked at the family. In all the years he'd known the Laceys, he'd never seen them so broken and lost.

"When you no longer have the one you love near you, and it seems as if heaven has taken the best of the souls placed here on earth, your spirit weeps. It weeps not because of the death of the body but for the spirit you once knew as your loved one. Don't cry for the person you've known as daughter, sister, or friend, but rejoice in knowing her pain and sorrow on earth are over. Rejoice with her in knowing she has a new and pain-free body, mind, and spirit. Rejoice in knowing God took the best and has created a place for her. God fills heaven with those he loves most. So when your heart feels heavy and you feel as if you can't go on without your loved one, know God has her in his arms, and she will cry no more.

"Rejoice! For this body is just a shell. Your loved one is far beyond the blue sky, in a far better place than what is here on earth. Rejoice! No more tears. No more pain. No more heartache. No more worry. No more suffering. Rejoice!"

Pastor Mullin's voice trailed off as he spoke over Tonya's still, quiet body.

Carmen knew Tonya was smiling down on her. She could enjoy being in the bosom of Christ with her baby in her arms. She imagined her sister singing in the heavenly choir, in a robe in the purest of white, lifting up the name of the savior. Pastor Mullin spoke about those pearly gates and streets paved in gold, and the joy of being in God's presence. Longing to be singing beside her sister once more, Carmen realized she'd never felt so alone.

As she looked upon the sleeping faces of Tonya and baby Cameron, she stepped forward on wobbly legs to say her last good-bye and leaned over and kissed them one last time.

Sister Peggy Frazier walked up behind her and touched her arm. "Don't you fret none, baby. God's got them now! Just enjoy the time you two shared together."

Carmen turned and gave Sister Peggy a tight hug, not wanting to let her go. "I know, but I'll miss her forever. She was all I had after Mom died."

"Chile, don't you be disencouraged. God's gonna work it out."

Sister Peggy really had a way with words. Carmen waved off the urge to correct her. She didn't have the heart to tell the poor woman there was no such thing as "disencouraged," but it didn't seem important anyway.

"Well, now you and your daddy have got to be there for each other. He'll need you to be strong. The two of you got to stick together like butter to a cold pan."

"Yes, ma'am," Carmen replied obediently, wondering if butter really stuck to a cold pan and why Sister Peggy didn't just say 'stick together like glue' like everybody else. Sister Peggy always knew how to make things better. Carmen knew why Tonya loved this woman so much.

Tonya always had been the strong one in the family. She was the one who'd kept everything together when their mother had died. How could Carmen possibly fill those shoes?

39

Sitting on the couch, holding the pearl-handled .38 in his right hand firmly to his temple, Keith contemplated ending his life. He thought about how life might have been had he never met Shayla.

"If I'd been a faithful husband to my wife, I'd be a happy father to my child today. Now I have no wife and no child—nothing but misery and guilt. Carmen was right; I should have been the one in the ground. Tonya didn't deserve that."

Keith's depression had spiraled out of control. He was at his lowest point and was sinking deeper into a dark place. His psychiatrist had increased his dose of Zoloft to the maximum of two hundred milligrams, but it only made him more agitated. He was experiencing bouts of diarrhea, had lost his appetite, and was feeling nauseous. The smell of his cologne alone made him sick. No matter how much water he drank, he couldn't get rid of his cottonmouth. To make matters worse, he hadn't slept in more than twenty-four hours. His body was exhausted, but he couldn't fall asleep.

He was about to pull the trigger when the phone rang. Not knowing why he felt the need to answer it instead of just shoot himself, he stood up and headed to the phone. Stubbing his toe on the end of the coffee table, he swore under his breath.

"Hello?" he spoke dryly into the receiver, trying to mask his irritation.

"George, come on, man. The game is about to start!" the voice on the other end yelled.

Taken aback, Keith looked at the phone before speaking. "Who? Oh, you must have the wrong number."

After he placed the receiver back in its cradle, he heard a commotion outside his front door. He hobbled over and opened it to see what was going on. He couldn't believe his eyes—standing on a moving pickup truck, a man was yelling into a microphone about coming to the Lord and giving your life to Jesus Christ. Annoyed, Keith quickly slammed the door. *People are straight crazy these days,* he thought. *Who ever heard of "Jesus on wheels"?* He laughed at his own joke. The thought of the little man screaming like he was selling ice cream made him laugh once more. Suddenly there was a knock on the door, which stopped Keith in his tracks. *Who could this be? No one knows I'm home,* he thought, as he cautiously approached the door. He opened the door to see two beautiful young women standing before him.

"Hello, sir. Have you received Jesus Christ into your heart?" the smaller of the two asked with a smile. He noticed they had Bibles in their hands.

"Oh, you're with 'Jesus on wheels,' huh?" Keith asked with a grin.

Not understanding his inside joke, the women looked at him with blank expressions.

"I'm Sister Margaret Steely and this is Sister Ava Lee. We're from Brighter Light Temple. We were led to speak to you about your soul salvation. Will you be ready for Jesus when he returns?" the heavier of the two ladies asked. Sister Lee looked to be younger than Sister Steely, but her makeup needed improvement. She wore eye brows that seem to have been drawn on her face with a black permanent marker. She wore a shade of pink lip gloss that was unflattering to her complexion. She would look a lot better if she just scratched the makeup and went natural.

Keith became impatient but refused to be rude to anyone representing a church. He had been raised with better sense than to be impolite to church people; he was almost sure it was some kind of sin to slam the door in the face of someone carrying a Bible.

"Sir, God has something better for you. Let me share something with you." Sister Lee opened her Bible and continued, "The Bible tells us to come unto him, all ye that labor and heavy laden, and he will give us rest. Son, you look tired and in need of a rest from the pressures of life, for in God there is life more abundantly."

Feeling tired and weak, Keith felt the need to sit down. He offered the ladies a seat. As he sat on the couch, he realized he had forgotten about the gun on the coffee table but was unable to hide it before one of the ladies spotted it.

"Sir, what were you about to do with that gun?" the smaller woman asked, clearly sensing Keith's troubled state.

Not wanting to lie, Keith lowered his head and mumbled, "End it all."

The two ladies stayed and spoke with him about allowing God to come into his life and replacing his anger with love and peace. They invited Keith to attend their church so he could give his life to Christ.

"Well, I don't have much life left, thanks to my mistakes in life and my death sentence."

Not fully understanding his plight, the women continued to extend their invitation and quoted scriptures on how God could give him eternal life.

Keith thought about his life after death and knew he didn't want to wake up in hell. "How can I make sure I don't die in sin? I've already done so much. It would take all year just to tell you about it. I haven't been to church in so long that God wouldn't even recognize my prayers. He's already forsaken me, so don't count on him forgiving me."

"Sir, God is a God of love and mercy. Your sins, no matter how great or small, can be forgiven if you sincerely ask him to forgive them." Sister Lee said.Opening her Bible, the woman flipped to 1 John 1:9 and recited, " 'If we confess our sins, He is faithful and just to forgive us our sins and to cleanse us from unrighteousness.' " She placed Keith's hand in hers and continued, "God is allowing you to come to him with a dirty and speckled life so he may make you clean."

Keith's heart began to soften as the women ministered to him about salvation. He had attended church regularly while he was growing up but had strayed somewhere after high school. He attended church only on certain holidays, and even those were few and far in between.

The two young ladies prayed with him and allowed him to cry as they spoke of all God had promised him, if he would give his life to him. Outside he still heard the little preacher shouting, "Repent and be baptized in the name of Jesus!"

Long after the two women from Brighter Light Temple had left, when he could no longer hear the preacher on the microphone, Keith felt hollow inside. Who could love someone like him? He couldn't be saved, because he could never surrender his life like Tonya had. The thought of his wife and son sent him into a convulsion as he cried for the lives of those taken. *Why wasn't it me? I should have been the one who died! They didn't deserve to die.* He didn't want to live his lifebeing constantly reminded of his misdeeds. He decided to do what he'd started to do before being interrupted.

He picked up the phone and called his dad, mother, and sister and left the same message. Knowing they'd all be at work, he banked on getting their voice mail. After saying his last good-byes and leaving messages of love and regret, Keith picked up the handgun and pressed the cold barrel to his temple. His hands shook as he mustered the courage to complete the deed. No matter how much he'd fought to get over the loss of his family, it didn't seem to be enough. He thought about what the woman from Brighter Life had said about dying and waking up in hell, but he'd have to take his chances. "Forgive me," he whispered, as he pulled the trigger and his mind faded to black.

40

Awakening to the sound of a beeping noise, Keith opened his eyes to see a fuzzy silhouette of a woman sitting in a chair near him.

"Tonya!" Keith said in a throaty whisper, getting the sleeping woman's attention. She jumped up as if she'd been set on fire. "Honey, you're awake!" she screamed, as she hugged him. Immediately she pressed the nurse's call light, shouting, "He's awake! He's awake!" Three nurses entered the room and began to ask him questions—"What is your name?" "What day is it?" "What year is it?" He tried to answer, but his lips were so dry that they cracked when he opened his mouth. Keith realized the woman wasn't Tonya after all, but his mother.

"Water," he pleaded in a raspy whisper.

As he tried to lean forward to accept a drink of water, his arms felt heavy, his body sluggish. He couldn't see clearly and wanted to know what was blocking his view. He grabbed at his face, unable to figure it out.

"Mr. Paris, what's wrong?" one of the nurses asked.

"I can't see very well."

"Sir, you've had a long journey. You've been in the hospital for four months. We didn't think you'd ever wake up. Do you remember how you got here?"

"Yeah, but why can't I see?"

"Mr. Paris, Dr. Donaldson will be in shortly to speak with you about your medical condition and your recovery process."

It must be really bad if she's afraid to tell me, he thought. Getting upset about being sent in circles, Keith decided to leave. "I'm out of here," he exclaimed. "I don't need this! Can't you just answer my questions?" He couldn't put the pieces together, nor could he will his sleeping legs to move.

"Honey, don't you remember how you got here?" his mother asked.

He settled down a bit to focus on her question and reflect on his memory of being brought to the hospital. "I must have gotten sick. Where's Tonya?"

"K.J., she's—"

"Go get my wife!"

"K.J., Tonya's dead. Don't you remember?"

Memories flooded his mind. He remembered his last hours with his wife, the son who didn't survive, and the gun he had put to his head. "I'm such a failure. I couldn't even do that right," he mumbled. He was sure he'd wake up on the other side.

"Thank God you didn't succeed," his mother said. "Son, I love you dearly. I was so hurt when I got your message on my answering machine."

"I need to leave now!" Keith demanded. Struggling to get out of bed left him spent; he couldn't understand how his life could have changed so drastically in such a short period of time.

One of the nurses rushed to his bedside, trying to calm him, while another ran from the room and quickly returned with a syringe that she injected into his IV line. Suddenly he found himself feeling calm and sleepy.

There was a gentle knock on the door. Keith recognized the familiar rap. His father always did rapid succession of five quick taps followed by one tap and five more with two quick taps behind. Keith turned to see his father's fuzzy silhouette standing in the doorway of his hospital room. He thought he would never see his father again on the night he attempted to take his life. He had left a message on his father's answering machine saying, "I know that I haven't been the best son, nor have I lived up to my expectations as a husband to Tonya, but I can no longer put the blame on you. It was my choice to halt our father-son relationship. It was my choice to cheat on my wife. It was my choice to not protect myself while being unfaithful, and giving my wife that virus that ultimately caused her demise. I have to take full responsibility for those things. I can't keep blaming the girl who gave it to me; she didn't have an obligation to me or my family. I know that now, which is why it is so hard to deal with. I might as well had taken a gun and killed my family. Nothing I can do can bring them back, but if I could trade places with them I would do it without any hesitation. I just want to let you know that I love you and that my actions do not reflect you as a father. It is too hard to go on. I just want to end that suffering. I can't live without my family, especially knowing I ultimately killed them. Please take care of Christine because she will need you. My mom is a strong woman, but nothing can prepare a mother after something like this, so I ask you to help her as well. If I could remove the pain that I know this will cause, I'd gladly do so. I love you and ask for your forgiveness."

Mr. Paris crossed the room and grabbed Keith by the shoulders and cradled his son as the two men embraced. Keith began to cry as he became overcome with a mixture of emotions from sorrow, joy, regret and relief all at once. Keith tried to speak, but his brain froze. He didn't know what to say, but he knew in that moment words were not needed. He felt like the prodigal son who had found himself back in his father's good grace.

A few minutes later, Dr. Donaldson spoke to Keith about his condition, explaining that the bullet to his head hadn't killed him but had lodged into his spine, rendering him paralyzed. His eyesight was failing him due to the gunshot wound. During his comatose state, he had contracted several opportunistic infections that had left his already compromised immune system acutely vulnerable.

He also had been treated for pneumonia, since he had been lying in bed for so long and had collected fluid in his lungs. Dr. Donaldson explained that he would have to continue his regimen of antibiotic therapy, along with his previous treatments initiated by Dr. Gipson. He added that Keith would have to go to a rehabilitation center, but Mrs. Paris insisted on taking her son home to care for him herself.

"Mrs. Paris, I'm not sure if you understand the seriousness of your son's conditions," Dr. Donaldson said. "It's a lot of work to take on. Do you have any help?"

"I cared for my son for eighteen years before I set him out into the world. What's so different now?"

"Well, for starters, he's more vulnerable than ever," the doctor said. "He's susceptible to infections, not to mention the risk of falling. Mrs. Paris, your son will need total care around the clock. Are you prepared to accept the liability?"

"My son is not a liability! I will not put my son in a nursing home!"

"Of course not. Mrs. Paris, a rehab center is a facility where he'll receive medical attention and—"

She raised her hand to cut him off. "I won't put my son in a rehab center."

Dr. Donaldson turned to Mr. Paris for support. Mr. Paris raised his hands in a gesture of surrender. He knew that when Mrs. Paris had a notion stuck in her head, it was there to stay.

Keith's mother remained steadfast; her refusal to send her son to a rehabilitation facility was evident when she signed the discharged papers and took him home.

—⁂—

As Keith sat up in his wheelchair, looking out the kitchen window, he wondered how long he'd be a burden to his mother. Tears trickled down his face. He'd never meant to hurt anyone, but by the looks of it, he'd done much more harm than good.-

Sensing her brother's sadness, Christine put her arms around Keith's neck and kissed his cheek. "Things will get better. Come on. Let me give you your eye drops."

Keith turned his chair toward his sister. "That's the least of my worries."

"K.J., please let me help you. Don't shut me out."

"Just put the drops in. I'm just tired, I guess. Don't take it personally."

Christine had come over every day since Keith had been discharged from the hospital. She felt it was her duty to help her brother. She couldn't allow her mom to carry the responsibility alone.

"I'm going to drive you to your doctor's appointment tomorrow. Wanna grab some lunch? We could have lunch in the park. It'd be great!"

Keith smiled at Christine; it took very little to please her. Her grin immediately lightened his mood. His weakness always had been the females in his life. He had doted over his little sister since the day she was born, and he still felt that love for her.

"Sure, lil sis."

Keith knew he'd enjoy going to the park with Christine. It reminded him of when he was younger and used to take her to the park. She had been such a grateful child. He loved being a big brother to Christine, because she was never a pest. The age gap was never a problem either; in fact it probably enhanced their relationship. At thirty-two, Keith enjoyed having a much younger sister, especially one who had so much energy and was so full of life. He was over-joyed when he was eleven and his parents had brought her home from the hospital. He had hated being an only child and had looked forward to coming home from school to the smell of baby lotion and the coos from his baby sister as he played with her and watched her grow. Keith had longed for the day when he would become a father, which ultimately only proved to be a burden on his marriage.

Looking at his now grown sister, he was glad he had her in his life. She looked as if their mother had bottled up her beauty and spread it all over Christine. Christine was in college, majoring in computer programming, some-thing Keith never had seemed to grasp; he had a tough time just figuring out how to use his cell phone. Always a bossy child, she never acted like the younger sister but constantly fussed over him. He often joked that between the two of them he didn't know who was the older sibling.

"KJ, I want you to talk to someone about your depression," Christine said.

"I'm cool."

"You're not cool. You tried to kill yourself."

"I don't need some shrink telling me I'm sick in the head."

"Counseling might do you some good. Just talk to someone," Christine pleaded.

"I'm fine. I'm not going to off myself, if that's what you're worried about."

"What changes things now? What makes everything different this time?"

"Chris, I'm OK. Let's just leave it at that."

"Why? So you won't have to make any promises not to harm yourself?"

"Look at me, Chris. What's left to take? I'm paralyzed, nearly blind, and have AIDS. I can't even use the bathroom on my own. How am I supposed to off myself without someone helping me?"

"KJ, please don't talk like that. You're scaring me."

"I'm just saying I'm too tired and weak to give it another try. Besides, if I was destined to die, I think I would have died then."

"Dr. Stuart is really good. I think you should give him a call. He might be able to help you."

"Give it a rest!" Keith barked.

"But K.J.—"

"Look, I'm too tired to fight with you. Let me think about it, OK?"

"OK," Christine said with tears in her eyes. She hated seeing her brother so miserable.

———※———

The next day, after his doctor's appointment and their visit to the park, Keith was exhausted. The phone rang. It was Brian he wanted to know if he and Jerry could talk to him, maybe come over later that evening. Keith didn't want to say no to his friends, but he didn't have the strength to see them.

"Let's plan to get together this weekend," he said. "I'm really tired today."

"Jerry and I wanted to let you know we're thinking about you, man. You can talk to us about anything, OK?"

"Sure. Look, I really need to get some rest." Keith didn't have the heart to show his irritation toward his old friend. He hadn't seen either of them since his suicide attempt. They hadn't visited him while he was in the hospital or since he'd been home. He wondered why they wanted to see him now.

"Later, man," Brian said.

"Yeah, later."

———※———

Placing a bouquet of white roses on Tonya and Cameron's grave gave Keith little solace as he sat with his head bowed. Sitting before his family, he ruminated on how his entire life had changed over the past two years since he'd lost his wife and son. He had come to grips with his loss, but moving on was difficult. It was time for him to forget his sorrows and self-pity and make amends for all the pain and grief he'd caused.

"Things would have been different for us if we had…if I had honored our vows," he said. "Please forgive me for my immoral behavior. I can only pray that you and Cameron are looking down on me without malice in your hearts. I can't change anything, but I promise to do everything I can to be reunited with you. If God can somehow forgive me for everything I've done, I promise to live out the rest of my days honoring him."

A sudden cold downpour chilled his bones. The sky lit up as lightning scattered through the heavens. As Keith prepared to leave, he felt a hand on his shoulder, which sent a warm sensation throughout his body. He knew this was a sign, as if God were saying, "All is forgiven."

Jerry and Brian rushed to help Keith out of the rain and into the car.

"Come on, man. We don't want you to get sick. It's starting to really pick up out here!" Jerry said, quickly locking the wheels on Keith's wheelchair as he and Brian helped Keith into the backseat.

Safely inside the car, Keith acknowledged a sense of wholeness as a feeling of peace settled over him. He felt closer to forgiving himself for the tragedy he had caused. He also felt blessed to have real friends like Brian and Jerry. Despite his foolish actions, they hadn't given up on him.

"Thanks, guys," he said. "I really needed to get out today. I hadn't seen the grave since the funeral two years ago."

"No problem, bro," Jerry said.

"Hey, let's go catch the game." Brian suggested.

"We're here for you, man. I just wish we'd been there before." Jerry glanced back at Keith as Brian headed toward Jerry's place. "We've been friends too long to just walk away from you. We're gonna see you through this."

Keith sat silently as tears formed in his eyes. He bit his bottom lip in an attempt to regain his composure. This was the first time he'd been certain in a long time about his bond with his longtime friends.

As the men sat on the couch in front of the TV, watching the game, Jerry broached the subject of Keith's suicide attempt. "Keith, I gotta know—why didn't you talk to us about what you were planning to do?"

Keith remained quiet as he rubbed the stubble on his chin and thought about out how to tell his friends how rejected he'd felt when they'd backed off from him when he'd told them he was HIV positive. Not wanting to offend them, or make them feel guilty, he didn't have a safe answer. *How do you tell your friends that they were part of what drove you to the point of no return?* Keith decided he couldn't blame them for his depression or suicide attempt.

"We don't blame you or want you to feel bad for not coming to us about your problem," Jerry said, "but you have to know that what you did hurt and affected everyone around you."

"I wasn't trying to hurt anyone, but you try dealing with what I was dealing with. I killed my wife and child; you tell me how I could live with that."

Brian raised his voice. "Man, that's a cop-out! Suicide doesn't solve anything. It just makes everyone else miserable. It's the most selfish thing a person can do."

"Whoa, man. Chill!" Jerry told Brian. "Let's give it a rest for now."

Jerry knew where the conversation was heading. Brian's older brother, Jeremy, had committed suicide six years ago. Jeremy was strung out on drugs; he'd been in and out of rehab so many times that it seemed hopeless. He eventually began to steal from his family to get money to feed his habit. One night, after a three-day binge, Jeremy jumped off a bridge into traffic below, which devastated his family. Traffic didn't stop for Jeremy, and when his body was discovered, it had been destroyed by fast-moving cars and trucks. There wasn't much left of Jeremy to bury, so his mother had him cremated. For months afterward, Brian avoided his family and anyone who reminded him of Jeremy. While Jeremy was alive, he couldn't seem to be able to get through to him. He had offered to pay for his treatment, but Jeremy was in denial and minimized his addiction. Even after six years, the feeling of having lost his brother was fresh in his mind.

The three friends sat and enjoyed the game until Keith asked to be taken home. He was having muscle spasms from sitting up for so long. The men agreed to meet on the weekend, which put a smile on Keith's face. It felt good to know his boys had his back.

On the way home, Keith couldn't ignore the odor that seeped from his clothes, and he knew his friends weren't able to ignore it either, but no one said a word about his little accident. The men assisted him inside as his mother cleared the way and wheeled him inside.

Brian and Jerry waved good-bye as Mrs. Paris took Keith to the rear of the house to clean him up. Christine thanked the men for spending time with Keith, telling them how much it meant to him. Brian watched as she grabbed a box of latex gloves and headed to bathroom to help her mother with Keith.

As the men drove away, they felt a sense of closeness with Keith that they had missed during their separation. Today seemed just like old times, as if they'd never missed a beat.

Keith reclined in bed after a long day with his friends. He reflected on his life and the pain and anguish he had endured over the past three years. He had to take responsibility for his life and stop blaming Shayla, Tonya, and his father. He had blamed Shayla for transmitting HIV to him. He had blamed Tonya for not keeping him home and working on their marriage. He had blamed his father for not teaching him how to be a loving husband, one who honored his wife. His father had stepped out on his mother, and history had repeated itself. He knew he'd eventually have to forgive himself. He surely could forgive his friends, but could he forgive himself? He bowed his head and prayed for God's love to overshadow him. He asked that the angels encamp around him as he journeyed through his life. He could no longer hold on to the anger and regret that had gripped him so tightly. Keith's eyelids grew heavy; he was exhausted. He remembered the preacher on the microphone outside his home the day he had wanted to end his life. He thought about how the man had yelled, "Repent, repent, repent!" As Keith drifted off to sleep, he uttered a word of repentance as God's love filled him with peace and tranquility.

Second Chance

Just to sleep and awake in a better place,
my soul could finally rest in peace.
I wanted to escape the pressures of life,
to know my problems would pass.
I contemplated my own desire
so I could have peace of mind.

As I waited for death to come,
I heard laughter in the air.
Was it me who laughed with joy?
I heard not joy in it but victory and deceit.
Someone was laughing as I slipped away.
My mind drifted; my body was still.
"You fool, I have you now!"
it mocked with a sinister laugh.

I heard my mother praying in the distance.
My father commanded for the enemy to step back
and loosen the hold he had on my life.
Somewhere near me God's voice spoke to me.
"I am not finished with you, my child.
Now go and do my will."

I opened my eyes to see my parents standing over me,
praising God for his victory over the enemy.
Truly God had given me a purpose to live.
Had I died, I would have lifted my eyes in hell,
but God's love set me free, giving me a second chance.

41

Abandoning the idea of sleep after the dream she'd just had, Carmen decided to get out of bed. Trying to decipher the meaning of the dream, she reflected on her sister and the years of wisdom she had bestowed upon her. She walked into her living room to look for pictures of her sister. Retrieving her family photo album from the bookshelf and looking at photos of Tonya's smiling face brought her peace of mind. Tonya's smile had been so radiant that it made people smile even if they didn't want to. Her personality had been so soft and loving that it was contagious. She made those around her gentle and loving people. The light in her eyes shone brighter than a flickering candle. Now that light had been put out, leaving Carmen in total darkness. A wave of anger overcame her as she thought about Tonya's life being cut short.

In the dream Carmen had seen Tonya standing above her with a pleasant smile. The vision of her sister was so sweet and angelic. Her voice was a whisper in Carmen's ear that echoed the very words of forgiveness Tonya once had uttered in life. The dream seemed so real that she had felt as if her sister were in the room with her.

Tonya's words vibrated in her ear. *It takes more strength to forgive than to walk around with anger in your heart.*

Those words were a great awakening to Carmen's inner being. She now understood the meaning of her sister's words regarding not holding on to hate and being able to forgive. She knew she had to forgive Keith in order to move forward. She had held so much hatred in her heart for the one person she deemed responsible for her sister's untimely demise.

Despite Tonya's wishes, however, Carmen found it difficult to let go. How could she forgive him? He had taken away her dearest friend. Her sister had meant everything to her, and now she was alone.

Carmen's lips quivered as tears sprung from her swollen eyes. They felt like heavy raindrops, reminding her of days when she had sat outside under a light sprinkling of summer rain. She cried for the loss of her sister and the pain of being an orphan. Tonya was more than a sister to her; she was her friend, her better half. Her tears flowed freely as she cradled a picture of her sister. No amount of time would ever heal the pain she felt from having lost her sister. Gathering her strength, Carmen began to pray. She needed God to heal her broken heart, but most of all she needed to purify her soul. Her father had told her that the body is the temple of God and that hate and has no place in that temple. Elder Lacey always had encouraged his daughters to walk in love and forgiveness. "Hate is like a festering sore. It will kill like cancer unless you let it go," he'd told Carmen when she had confided how she felt about Keith after Tonya's death.

The atmosphere in the room changed. She felt compassion in her heart for Keith and was no longer angry about Tonya. She knew her sister was in a better place. She picked up a pen and jotted down her innermost thoughts.

My Burden

One day, while on my knees, I prayed.
I cried, begged, and swayed.
I asked, "Why me? Why me?"
Such a heavy cross to bear.
I felt as if my life would suddenly end,
for I was in such despair.

No greater pain could I feel
than to lose someone so dear.
My tears would not stop flowing,
nor would my heart stop breaking.
Then quietly a voice so calm, so serene
whispered words so peaceful to me.

My soul stopped stirring
and listened with intent,
as the voice spoke these words to me.
"I will never give to you more than you can bear."

I stood in the center of the room.
The tears stopped flowing,
and I could see much clearer.
My loss wasn't a loss at all
but a bridge to cross over to the next life.
Truly my joy was coming in the morning.

42

Waking up in the middle of the night, with a chill down his spine and feeling feverish at the same time, Keith was unable to stop his body from quivering. He had been at this very place twice before and knew he'd contracted pneumonia again. Keith had suffered his first bout of pneumonia while he was in the hospital after his suicide attempt. The second incident occurred a year later when he had caught a simple cold that developed into pneumonia. He remembered that time vividly. He knew he'd have to get to the hospital, but he didn't have the strength to call anyone for help.

Looking at her watch, Christine wondered why Keith wasn't up and dressed. He had made it a routine of being ready for his doctor's appointments without being coaxed. When she had walked into the kitchen, she had expected to find him in his wheelchair, sitting by the window and waiting for her, but his usual spot was empty.

As she entered his room, she saw Keith from the doorway. He was lying in bed, taking slow, uneven breaths. He looked pale; the blood had drained from his face; and his lips had a bluish tint. She rushed to his side. "KJ, what's wrong?" she asked him. "You don't look well. I'm going to call an ambulance."

His last bout of pneumonia had been treated with antibiotics after he'd been hospitalized. At that time the doctors alerted him of his dangerously low cell count. Infection at this level was almost always fatal; he'd gotten through it but not without the prayers of the members of New Covenant Full Gospel, led by Elder Lacey. Now he was back in the same place.

Drifting in and out of sleep, Keith was too weak to call out for assistance. Glancing at the clock, he noted it was 3:20 a.m. It would be at least five more hours before anyone would come in to check on him.

As he drifted in and out of consciousness, he saw a vision of Tonya standing near his bed. She wore her hair down and donned a beautiful full-length gown that flowed freely, as if the wind were blowing behind her. Clutched to her bosom was a smiling baby boy. Tonya didn't speak but just stood before him, smiling down on him. As Keith reached out to her, she moved back, as if floating slowly away from him.

"Don't go!" Keith yelled.

Tonya quickly vanished.

"No, don't go!" he protested.

"K.J., who are you talking to?" his mother asked, adding, "I'm right here," as she stroked his face.

No longer able to see through his failing eyes, Keith realized he was in his room at home, with his mother leaning over him. He didn't see the smiling faces of Tonya or baby Cameron. Was it a vision or simply a mirage?

Bringing him breakfast was Christine's duty. She always made sure he had something in his stomach before he took his medicine. She tapped on the door before entering the room.

"Wake up, sleepyhead!"

When he didn't reply as usual, she came closer.

"K.J., wake up."

Keith was too weak to talk; he was delirious and feverous. He was soaking wet, his body trembling uncontrollably.

Turning on her heels, Christine ran to get her mother. "Call nine-one-one!"

"What's wrong?"

"It's K.J."

"Is he breathing?"

"Yes but barely. Tell them to hurry!"

En route to the hospital, Keith heard the medical crew calling in their estimated arrival time and giving the hospital staff a report on his status—it didn't sound good.

I don't want to go like this…I haven't said good-bye to my loved ones, he thought while lying on the stretcher. "Where's my mother?" he asked the paramedics, struggling to speak.

"Sir, your family will meet you at the hospital. Try to relax. You don't want to use up any more energy than necessary."

Keith almost asked the man where his wife was until he remembered that Tonya was dead. Tears flowed from his lifeless eyes as he thought about everything he had endured and lost.

"Sir, we're almost there. Hang in there!"

43

Keith found himself back in the hospital with a temperature of 104 degrees. His mother immediately had called 911 when she realized he was in trouble. He was now hooked up to IV lines that ran fluids and antibiotics through his veins. He had lost days from the time he was brought to the hospital until now. Lying in bed confused and disoriented hadn't been Keith's plan for his life. Feeling cold and clammy, he couldn't stop his body from shaking. He went from feeling feverish, with sweat dripping down his body, to being as cold as the arctic snow. He felt achy and restless. No matter how much his mother and sister rearranged his pillows, repositioned his lifeless legs, and pulled him up in bed when slid down, he couldn't get comfortable.

He couldn't focus on what his sister was saying, but he knew she was at his bedside the entire time. Knowing that Christine rarely left his side brought him comfort. He couldn't see her, but her voice was filled with a reassurance that told him everything would be all right. Her diligence in sitting with him confirmed that he was still loved.

Keith's visitors included his family, Jerry and Brian, and his father-in-law, Elder Lacey, who prayed for him before leaving his room. Keith was pleased to see his father-in-law, which validated that Elder Lacey didn't hate him after all. He knew he'd never get that from Carmen, so he sent a word of apology to her with Elder Lacey. It felt good to see that his family and friends still cared for him, despite his misdeeds.

Jerry and Brian came every day after work to sit and reminisce about their past. Keith didn't have the heart to tell the guys he'd long forgotten most of the things they talked about. Jerry tried to make him remember someone name Rain. Apparently she had stopped by to see him while he was unconscious. He didn't remember her, even when they described her to him. He could hardly remember Jerry and Brian, let alone people from his past. He once called Jerry "Brian"; he kept getting things mixed up. The simplest things were no longer simple. It really frustrated him when he couldn't get his brain to work; sometimes he felt like his mind wasn't wired right or was misfiring.

The men looked at each other and shrugged. At least he knew they were there. Was he losing his mind? Brian suggested that maybe because he couldn't see, he had mistaken them, but even he didn't believe that.

Keith was growing increasingly agitated regarding memory lapses and lashed out at the men when they tried to jar his memory. They tried to help him to remember people they had known for years, but nothing was clicking. He couldn't get it through their thick skulls that he had no interest in going down memory lane. He could barely remember what he had eaten for breakfast. He did, however, remember that his sweet grandmother had come by to see him. She looked just as youthful as the last time he'd seen her, but something was different about her visit. She didn't stay and chat with him like she had when he was younger. He wished he could spend more time with her, but she seemed to be in such a hurry.

Keith's father stopped by the hospital every night before the end of visiting hours. He didn't stay long; he couldn't stand seeing his son in such a state. He came by even when Keith no longer recognized him, calling him "mister." It was sad for his family and friends to watch Keith's mind deteriorate before their eyes.

"Grandma Rose came to visit me last night," Keith told Christine. "She didn't stay long. She just came to see how I was doing."

"K.J., Grandma Rose couldn't have come to see you last night."

"Yeah, she told me she misses me. I miss her too. Gotta go visit her when I get better."

"K.J., Grandma Rose has been dead for almost ten years."

Keith became quiet then mumbled, "Well, she sure did stop by to check on me. She even called me 'Toot,' like she did when I was little."

Christine's mouth dropped open. There was no denying this; only Grandma Rose had called him "Toot." If their deceased grandmother had visited him, it could only mean one thing.

The family came to realize that Keith's health had taken a turn for the worse when his cognitive levels became gravely affected. One evening, while his mother and sister sat at his bedside, Keith spoke in garbled and broken English.

"Gimme…gimme," Keith said over and over, hoping someone would understand that he wanted a drink of water. Becoming frustrated, he banged on the bedside table. What Keith heard wasn't what he'd intended to say. Why couldn't he get his brain to work?

His behavior scared his family; they didn't know this stranger lying in bed. Keith never had been this aggressive toward them. Why was he so angry?

—w—

Mrs. Paris spent her days preparing for her son's funeral by calling Keith's life insurance company and meeting with the funeral-home director to choose the dreaded casket and arrange the service program. Halfway through getting things in order, she broke down in tears. No mother should have to bury her child. There are no instruction manuals to prepare someone for such a heart-breaking task. She agonized as she looked through his pictures and decided which ones to use for the program.

The doctors were frank in letting her know that Keith's cardiac output was only at 40 percent, and he was getting weaker by the day. It was evident that his body had become extremely weak. Just sitting up in bed was a job in itself; after only twenty minutes of being in an upright position, he was exhausted. How long would it be before his heart failed him?

Christine spent two hours trying to find the perfect suit for Keith. She eventually chose a dark-blue suit and a matching tie. She found a white shirt trimmed in sky blue to set off the dark-blue suit. She found a matching gold tie clip and cuff links and had the set engraved with his initials. Spending time shopping kept her mind occupied and helped her forget the real reason for her shopping.After choosing her brother's burial attire, Christine decided to take a break. Taking a seat at the food court, she pulled out the book of poetry Keith had given her a few months prior. She had promised him that she would keep it close to her heart. As she thumbed through the book, she came across one that caught her eye. The poem described Keith's feelings about his situation.

Forbidden Fruit

So tempting and tantalizing to the eye.
The warning label I question—"Why?"
The way she sashays and sways
in my memory I constantly replay.
With beauty and youth on her side,
my heart aches to discover what lies inside.
More than the eye can tell,
my desires are out of bounds, my sense of reason fails.

This forbidden fruit—I take a bite.
So sweet and juicy, it waters in my mouth.
Surely no poison could it hold,
yet the warning label burns in my soul.
Too late to turn back, no future ahead,
once you partake of that forbidden fruit.

Christine cried as the realization that soon her brother would be gone sunk in. She'd never imagined the day would come when she'd no longer have her big brother around to look out for her. Reality wasn't painting a pretty picture; she'd rather live in a state of denial. Why did Keith have to get sick like this? Why wasn't there a cure for this disease? With all the research she kept hearing about, why couldn't they find a cure before she lost her brother?

44

"K.J. doesn't even remember us," Brian told Jerry.

"I know. At first I thought it was because of the medication. He's on some pretty heavy-duty stuff. He keeps calling me 'Steve.' "

Brian shook his head. "Does he even know a Steve?"

"Probably not. I keep trying to help him remember all the things we've done together, but he just keeps saying, 'We did that?' "

The men felt as if they'd lost their friend for good. The trio had been through so much;

they'd shared so many years together, helping each other through college, celebrating weddings, and supporting one another during the deaths of loved ones. When things had gotten too hard to handle alone, they'd had one another's backs. They'd spent so much time together that they seemed inseparable. They couldn't understand how all that time could be wiped away from Keith's memory, like a bad VHS tape.

"Is this what AIDS does to you erase the memory of your life?" Brian asked. "When I spoke with his mom last week, she told me he doesn't even remember that Tonya died."

"Christine said he got some sort of virus that attacked his brain. That's probably why he doesn't remember anything."

"His mom asked me to be a pallbearer," Brian said with tears in his eyes. "A pallbearer. I was his best man when he and Tonya got married."

"Yeah, she asked me too. I couldn't turn her down, but who wants to bury their best friend?"

"I know. I can't stop thinking about that. The last funeral I went to was my granddad's, and he was eighty-seven years old. We're too young to be thinking about burying our friend."

"Let's head over to see him tonight," Jerry said. "Who knows how much time we have left?"

The two sat in silence as they considered the impact Keith's death would have on their lives. Since college the three men had been as close as brothers. What would their lives be like without him?

—m—

Sitting in the hospital at her brother's bedside, Christine read him poems from his book of poetry. She particularly enjoyed the love poems he had written to Tonya years ago. He even had included a poem about her brown eyes. *He was very romantic*, she thought, as she continued to read to him. Suddenly Keith's breathing began to change. Not knowing if he was asleep, Christine touched his shoulder. "K.J., are you OK?"

Keith didn't respond. His rapid, irregular breathing was the only indication that he was still alive. Christine became fearful; she had heard about the last breath people took, which sounded a lot like what Keith was doing now. She flipped open her cell phone and called her parents as well as Keith's pastor and his two best friends. She didn't like the sound of this new ragged, raspy breathing; he couldn't possibly live like this much longer. He signed his Do Not Resuscitate orders months ago, which deemed that no one tries to save his life if he died naturally. This was the hardest thing that she could handle. No one would come to his rescue if he decided to take his last breath. The nurse had prepared the family for what was to come, but even that didn't make it any easier. His oxygen saturation rate was low and fading fast as he struggled with each breath.

"K.J.?" she said. "Can you hear me?"

Keith was far from her. He no longer heard her or felt her presence. He was trying to find himself through a fog of confusion. He felt as if he were off balance and falling. He heard muffled words behind him, but it sounded as if whoever was calling him was far away. Keith's attention was focused on something or someone coming toward him. He couldn't make out the silhouette, but whoever it was didn't seem to be in a hurry. Keith waited.

Christine began to cry; she knew her brother was leaving her fast. She sobbed as she buried her face in his chest. His body was rigid and still. His body was still warm from the fever, but his hands were ice cold. He struggled with every inhalation, and his exhalations were long and uneven. Christine touched Keith's face, leaned over, and gently kissed his cheek. His jaw was locked, and his mouth was wide open, as if to ensure he received all the oxygen he could get. Keith let out a long sigh, then nothing. Christine shook him, desperate to bring him back. His breathing restarted on its own, and he continued to take irregular, ragged breaths. He experienced cycles of brief apnea that made it seem as if he had slipped away, but each time he started to breath on his own again.

Christine reached for the suction tube and cleared Keith's mouth of the buildup of phlegm. He was too weak to swallow his own saliva and probably would choke if she weren't vigilant about keeping his mouth suctioned. She placed the eye drops in his eyes, cleaned his mouth, and put some droplets in his mouth to keep his oral mucosa moist. Since he was no longer eating or drinking, his mouth was continually dry. She applied Vaseline to a Q-tip and rubbed it across his lips. Christine regressed to the little girl who always had looked to her older brother for comfort. As she wiped his brow with a cool washcloth she wondered, *Who will look after me now?*

"K.J., don't go," she cried out. Please don't leave me!"

Keith's family gathered around his bed, praying and comforting one another. Pastor Mullin came as soon as he was called, bringing Elder Lacey with him. Elder Lacey led the group in prayer, holding on to Christine at the foot of Keith's bed. Jerry and Brian stood next to the bed, watching their friend as he prepared to make his exit. Christine couldn't recall a time when the three of them weren't together. They had proven to be true friends to the end.

The hospital staff was very understanding, allowing the entire family to come to see Keith, with his father standing at the head of his bed. Women from the church came pray with the family, give a word of comfort, and hold his relatives' hands during their time of need. Keith's father stood next to his son's bed with red and puffy eyes as he watched his son prepared to make his final transition. His mother sat in a chair placed next to the bed holding her son's hand. She didn't want a minute to pass without having contact with him. As helpless as she felt, this gave her a peace of mind to know that he knew that she was near.

Looking up, Christine couldn't believe her eyes. Standing in the doorway was Carmen. She hadn't seen her since Tonya's funeral, the day when she had flown into a rage and attacked her brother. Was she coming to make good on her promise?

Carmen walked over to Keith's bed, leaned over, and whispered in his ear, "I forgive you. Go in peace."

Elder Lacey held his daughter as she cried over the loss of her sister, nephew, and brother-in-law. Carmen seemed small and fragile in her father's arms as her body trembled uncontrollably.

A single tear slid down Keith's cheek. Had he heard Carmen, even though his mind had taken him somewhere else?

Elder Lacey took out his handkerchief and wiped away Keith's tear. "God is just wonderful. He'll meet you wherever you are. Whether you're healthy or sick, oriented or confused, God will meet you where you are."

Christine touched Carmen's shoulder. "I'm glad you came. I'm sure he heard you."

"I'm glad I came as well. It's what Tonya would have wanted."

Carmen felt someone's hand on her back. The touch was light, warm, and engaging. She turned to acknowledge who was reassuring her then noticed no one was standing behind her. At that instant she felt confirmation that Tonya was pleased with her. It was exactly what she needed for her heart to heal.

The door to the hospital room opens as a group of church members files out and a new group comes in, it was literally becoming a revolving door. This had been happening all day. The last person on earth that Christine thought would come to see Keith walks in. Christine raises her eyebrow in surprise as Rain makes her way through the crowded room and approaches Keith's bed. She leans over and places a kiss on his forehead, stands up straight and pulls a young girl close to him. The girl, who looked to be about twelve years old and the spitting image of Rain, leans over a kisses Keith's cheek. "Good-bye daddy" she whispered.

Christine mouth dropped open in disbelief. The child looked like Rain, but she has Keith's eyes and complexion, although his skin had darkened over the years. She also had his lean build. It didn't take a genius to put this together. Mrs. Lacey also sat in shock. She had no idea that Keith had a child. Christine remembered how Rain looked at a younger age, with long black curls that bounced when she walked. This was the pas Rain standing before her.

"Is this Keith's daughter?" she asked Rain.

"Yes, this is Gabrielle."

"Did…did he know?" she stammered.

"He did." She looked back at Keith for reassurance before adding, "He didn't want to hurt Tonya."

"Why not tell his family? Why not let us know this child?" Mrs. Lacey asked. She was never the one to turn a child away. She knew how hard it was for her when she gave birth to Christine and how her ex-husband treated her. He made it known that she was not his child and it was hurtful.

"I'm here now grandma. I would love to get to know my dad's family."

"Well, you've certainly got your dad's height." Mrs. Lacey said, giving the girl a once over.

"I'm Christine. I guess that would make me your aunt."

"Nice to meet you Aunt Christine. My dad told me all about you and grandma. I feel like I've known you all my life."

"And how long has that been?" Christine asked.

"I'm ten and a half."

Mrs. Lacey gave the child a big hug. "God always leave us with something to hold on to, doesn't he?"

45

Keith finally felt at peace after asking for forgiveness and allowing the people who meant the most to him back into his life. For too long he had abandoned his family and friends, and now they all had forgiven him and had come today so he could make amends. It was as if a weight had been lifted from his shoulders, and hissoul felt light as a feather. He also felt a surge of forgiveness, and his feelings toward Shayla changed from hatred to compassion. He knew he couldn't continue to hate her, because then she'd win. He had realized that he too had been at fault for the peril in which he had placed his family. He could only hope that he'd done enough to make amends. Tonya had been such a loving and forgiving person that he didn't deserve her. He had hoped for forgiveness from God, but how could God look past everything he had done?

If he could go back in time and live his life over, he'd be the husband Tonya deserved, the man he had vowed to be on their wedding day. He'd be a good father to his son and spend more days in church and less time hanging out with the fellows. If he could just have that time to do over, he'd be a better son to his father, a better brother to his sister, and a better provider to his family. Keith silently laughed at the calamity of the matter and shook his head. *That's the funny thing about life*, he thought. *You only get one shot.*

Sensing a different presence in his room, he opened his eyes. His eyesight was suddenly clear; he saw things he hadn't been able to see since that fateful day when he had awoken from his coma. That was only one regret he'd lived with, losing his eyesight after his failed suicide attempt. Instead of ending his life, he'd only made matters worse; he'd become an invalid. He hated having to depend on his family to take care of his every need.

His family and friends were gathered around his bed. He saw Christine crying as she sat at his bedside. Next to her was Carmen, whose aura exuded love and peace. Keith didn't know when or how his relationship with Carmen had changed so drastically, but now that he was back in her good graces, he'd do his best to stay there. Jerry and Brian stood at the foot of his bed, looking somber and resigned. No one was joking around as usual, which dampened Keith's spirits. He'd have to work harder to cheer them up. He also knew he had to work on being a better friend. Now that he had his eyesight back, they could hang out together like old times. Elder Lacey always had been the pillar of the family. He led the group in prayer as they bowed their heads. Keith wanted to reach out to them and tell them everything would be all right, but he could only watch quietly.

In the background, standing behind his mother, he saw Tonya once again. She held their son, who smiled as he slept in her arms. Keith wanted to know why he hadn't been able to see her again until now. Tonya, like before, looked gorgeous; she wore her hair down, in soft curls that rested on her shoulder. She wore a beautiful, long, flowing white gown that seemed to blow with a slight breeze, although there wasn't a breeze in the room. Wondering if this would be like the mirage he'd seen before, he prayed she wouldn't leave him. Puzzled, Keith wondered what this apparition meant.

Stretching an arm toward him, Tonya beckoned for him to come to her as she slowly distanced herself from those standing in the room. She looked so angelic, with her slight smile and a twinkle in her eyes.

Keith reached to grab her hand, not wanting her to leave him as she had before. In doing so, he realized he now could move his formerly lifeless legs. In awe he looked down to see a pair of healthy, well-formed legs. He didn't feel the pain he'd felt whenever he'd tried to move too quickly. He thought about the times he'd fallen from his wheelchair because his mind had played tricks on him, telling him he could walk. Cautiously testing his legs, Keith stood up. He looked at Tonya in amazement that he hadn't fallen to the floor. As he took a step forward to test his new limbs, he felt very light, as if he were floating. He grinned broadly; this was a day of miracles. The doctors had told him that he wouldn't walk again and that his eyesight wouldn't improve, but he had proven them all wrong. Had he defied medical science? Was this the miracle he had so longed and prayed for?

Like a toddler walking on his own for the first time, Keith took a wobbly step toward his wife and child as she serenely beckoned him to follow her. To his astonishment his gait was much sturdier than he'd imagined, and he felt a sense of triumph. Unlike those times before, he was now able to reach out and touch Tonya. Keith looked into her eyes and felt an overwhelming sense of peace and tranquility.

Fearing she might slip away, Keith clutched Tonya's hand tightly. She held his hand securely in hers as she led him toward that bright, incandescent light.

At last he understood.

Acknowledgments

I'd like to give thanks to my Lord and savior, Jesus Christ, for giving me the opportunity and desire to spread this message of life, love, and forgiveness. To my daughter Shay, thank you for being understanding when Mom was too busy writing to chat. Thank you, thank you, thank you to my parents for their support. A million thanks to Beverlyn and Fred Dean (my other parents) for offering their love and support over the years and never giving up on me. A shout-out to my sister Bernie, my partner in crime, and my sister Cindi, the queen of neologisms—I learned from the best! A special thank-you to Joey Craig for aiding me and sharing this dream with me; I love you lots! Charday, thanks for reading the first draft and giving priceless feedback and for being a great niece. Thanks to Janice and Almeta for being great sisters and sharing my life. To my brothers Anthony, Darnell, and Marshall, thank you for my great memories of having big brothers—love ya! You all have a very special place in my heart. To my host of nieces, nephews, aunts, uncles, and cousins, please don't feel left out—you know I love you to pieces!

Bishop and First Lady Leo S. Lewis, thank you for allowing God to use you to help me grow into the woman I am today. Yes, Bishop, I got it! Thanks to two very special women in my life, Dr. Doris C. Anthony and Carla Johnson, for helping me to grow under their wings at GMCA. It's no wonder I became a great nurse—I've had such fine examples. Oliver Anderson, a very dear friend, I'll always hold a special place in my heart for you. Thank you for always having the time to listen to me and giving me mounds of advice. Rod (Spider Man), thanks for pushing me to finish this book. To the SATP veterans who have listened to me educate weekly on the subject of HIV and AIDS, thanks for your valuable input. Thanks to Lakesia Jackson, my friend since childhood—love ya, girl! Dennis James (wherever you are), thank you for encouraging me to write. Tony Stanford, thanks for sharing with me your gift of writing. To my divas Frankie and Elese, and my friend Dr. B., thanks for being real! To my girl Diane Peterson, thanks for your support and remember to keep your dreams close to you. To Lakeisha Sneed, my sister from another mother, thank you for just being you! A special thanks to Daphne, Edith, Margaret, Emma J., and Valerie for being such sweet and giving people.

I'd like to give a special shout-out to my friends since 1994, Charita Spearman, Clevette Tucker; my shipmates (94IO56), fellow corpsmen of class 94130, including Allen Chesney; my Portsmouth Naval Hospital cohorts (1994–96); and my niece Urlisa—hang in there, sailor!

In loving memory of my brother, Mallie "Cricket" Shavers (December 21, 1950–April 6, 2008); I love and miss you dearly. To my friends Gary Lee, Ana Shaw, Tan Giles, and Jerry Brown, forever loved and never forgotten; RIP.

And last, thank you to all my family and friends who have simply played a part in my life, giving me tons of material, laughter, and moments that make me say, "Hmm."

www.ingramcontent.com/pod-product-compliance
Lightning Source LLC
Chambersburg PA
CBHW031955240626
47153CB00003B/993